D

The Deepwater Trilogy

Deepwater Black
Deepwater Landing
Deepwater Angels

Deepwater Black

Ken Catran

Hodder
Children's
Books

a division of Hodder Headline plc

Contents

Author's note

Deepwater Black is a science fiction story. The area called 'Colour-space' is part of that fiction, but much of the universe is unknown – so something even more fantastic might lie waiting to be discovered.

Light speed and the distances between planets and stars are accurate. Voice-ac computers and gene-cloning are practically a reality today. Earth's first solar colony on another planet will certainly be Mars and terraforming (adapting a planet's environment to support life) is already a quite advanced scientific theory. The asteroid belt between Mars and Jupiter is thought to be rich in minerals and may one day be mined. Ceres (where Bren was born) is the largest asteroid in this belt – a quarter of the size of our moon.

Space is infinite. It goes on without end and we believe the universe does curve in a circle. To give an idea of the distances involved, let us think of Earth's solar system as our own backyard and our galaxy, the Milky Way, as our suburb. Even travelling at light-speed (three hundred thousand kilometres a second!), it would take more than one hundred thousand *years* just to go from one end of our galactic suburb to the other!

There is no life in outer space that we know about. But again, considering how much of this endless black ocean waits to be explored, anything is possible.

Once, we thought there was no life in the deepest part of the ocean. Now we know differently. Life exists there as it does everywhere, adapted to its environment.

So perhaps, somewhere, the trites and amebs and other space creatures lie waiting for the first explorer . . .

1   *The girl from nowhere*

A strange girl with a laser rifle. I'm telling this story from when she first appeared. She was strange because of how she looked and what she said – and because nobody else could see her.

It was on one of those hot, boring school afternoons that go on for ever. Everybody was half asleep, even Ms Booth, and I didn't hear the classroom door open. As I found out later, this girl didn't use doors sometimes. She was just there, standing by the blackboard, looking at me.

She had on a grubby silver-grey track suit and a silver-grey headband over long, thick, dark-blonde hair, streaked with red. There was a little headset thing clipped on this. She had a strong face and one of those wide, smiling mouths. But she wasn't smiling. Slung over one shoulder was a long purple metal tube with a hand-grip in the middle and flattened at one end into a set of controls. She looked tired and pale.

Ms Booth didn't take any notice of her. That was funny. I thought maybe she was from an acting group or one of those advertising gimmicks and she'd be handing out takeaway vouchers.

I glanced at the kid next to me. Glyn Evans wants to be a rugby league player and reckons he'll make a million bucks in sponsorship deals. He was yawning. I nudged him and pointed at the girl. He looked at her then back at me.

'What, Milkybar?' he whispered.

'That girl,' I said and pointed. All the time she was staring straight at me, level and steady, like she was coming to a decision. 'The blonde-and-red-haired one in the grey track suit with something that looks like a gun.'

Glyn followed my pointing finger again, then looked back at me. He must have remembered conning me two days ago with that bank robbery story. He just smiled, rolled his eyes and gently tapped his head. On the other side of the room, Denie Miles gave me a frowning look, but she was always doing that – and she didn't look at the girl either.

The girl just stood there, one hand on the strap of her gun. A paper pellet stung my ear and I turned. Behind me, Meatgrinder showed his teeth and held up three fingers. Meatgrinder is big and mean and runs a protection racket from his mum's video shop. And he sits right behind so *he* should have seen her – but he just put up three fingers again and closed his eyes.

I made to nudge Glyn again and a hand touched my shoulder. The girl was there. Close up, she had smudges under her eyes like Mum gets from too much overtime, and one big silver earring. There was a name printed in black letters over the pocket of her track suit: YOONA.

'This is a long prex, Reb,' she whispered.

Prex – what the hell was a prex? And Reb? Everyone calls me Robbie or Milkybar. And why was nobody taking any notice of her? Glyn was reading his book, Ms Booth looking out of the window and then, *right then*, I realised that nobody else could see her.

And right then I should have jumped up and freaked out and even yelled my head off because all this was just too weird! But something inside stopped me. And she must have read my thoughts because her hand rested on my shoulder like she understood. Her voice was urgent, tired and desperate.

'Prex, Reb, pre-existing? It's just another bad memory trip, but try and pull yourself out because we need you—'

'All right, let's wrap it up and don't forget the lab trip, Monday, nine *sharp*,' said Ms Booth. Everyone came awake very quickly and headed for the door. And the girl had gone,

4

just like that, but I could still feel her hand on my shoulder. Then my memory of her seemed to click off, too.

Our playground is a big patch of grey. Glyn and I always raced each other for the bike sheds. This time he won and was up and pedalling with a 'yayyh Milkybar' out of the school gates. A hand grabbed my bike and swung me round. Meatgrinder pushed his face up close and snarled like a mad dog.

'Listen, Milkybar-Mikkelson, you owe three games. By tomorrow it's four games and then I'm kicking ass.'

'Yeah, Mikkelson, get the message, kicking ass,' said the creep Reeboks, his sidekick, and they both headed off out the school gates after Glyn. He was two games behind.

Denie Miles was on her bike, looking at me, then at Meatgrinder. She shook her head and cycled off. It was OK for Denie to be like that. She did self-defence and when Meatgrinder tried his little act, he walked funny the rest of the day, like his underpants were too tight.

I headed home. Home is at the end of a cul-de-sac. One of those development projects where everything is flat and every second house has a garden gnome on the lawn. We have four bedrooms, kitchen/dining, family room, bathroom, etc. 'We' are younger brother David, sister Sarah, Mum and Dad, and the bank owns 38 per cent of us. Mum is a supermarket manager and Dad got laid off – he does anything he can. David is computers, Sarah is netball and both are a total pain I am stuck with.

I broadsided into our drive and up to the garage. I got off the bike and Yoona stepped in front of me. She looked just the same, but even more tense.

'The trites hit us again today. We've got jel in the ventilation systems and there's a solunk ahead too big to go round.' She rattled off all this like a shopping list. 'Get out of this prex, Reb, I need you on Deepwater.'

'What's a prex?' I said. 'And what's Deepwater – and who are you?' All at once she looked really puzzled – and scared.

'Robbie!' yelled Dad from the house, 'Bike out of the drive!'

Yoona was gone. This time my memory didn't click off, and I didn't freak either. I just looked around, then headed inside and her voice fast-forwarded in my mind . . . need you . . . need you . . .

I watched telly until dinner-time. It was Mum's late work night so Dad was cooking. I got into the usual hassles with David and Sarah about changing channels and who could use the tape deck. And I still wasn't scared.

I should have been scared – I should have been climbing the wall! I wasn't on medication or anything and strange girls in grey track suits don't just appear out of thin air. And I still had this deep-down little feeling that all this was OK, that it *should* be happening.

We had dinner and Mum came home looking more tired than usual. I know we're short of money because I made a joke to Dad about selling the car, and he made one back about selling my bike – and he wasn't joking.

It was like the girl Yoona didn't really exist, that she was a film I'd seen, or a story I'd read in a book. I did some homework and went to my bedroom to read. No more kids in grey track suits showed up. I even looked at myself in the mirror and it was me all right. Black hair, sharp face, always looked hassled, says Ms Booth. Like a fox-terrier, says Glyn, pure Celtic and lovable, says my nice Mum. So why hadn't I told her and Dad what happened?

Not only because I wasn't scared; it just felt like I should lock it in. It's like knowing there are other countries in the world without talking about them or ever seeing them.

My mum came in. 'Dad was joking about selling your bike, kiddo,' she said. 'We'll get by.'

I nodded and she gave me a little nudge. 'Your cop show is starting.'

'Ah, Mum, it's no good since Sergeant Dorcas got run over,' I said.

'He didn't get run over, he left the show because they

6

wouldn't pay him enough,' she said. Mum read that in a magazine and believes in the truth. 'Catch you later.'

She got up and left. I shut my eyes and a horrible feeling of blackness suddenly churned around, like all the tension of this thing had caught up with me. Then I was grabbed by the shoulder very hard and jerked round. It was the blonde girl, Yoona, out of nowhere again.

'Reb!' She was shouting, very uptight. 'I have to do this!'

Something punched into my arm and a million bright colours exploded in my body. My eyeballs bounced like footballs and I crashed back as though hit by a bus – but my bed was suddenly hard and narrow.

'Get up!' yelled Yoona.

There was an awful taste of mouldy rags in my mouth and I felt I was made of wet paper. Yoona pulled me up; she was very strong.

'Come on, up, stand up,' she shouted.

There was a hard crash from somewhere. I saw a metal floor underneath and legs – my legs – dressed in the silver-grey track suit bottoms. The room was big and long, and ahead of me a metal staircase ended at the ceiling.

'Get going, get to the stairs,' she yelled, unslinging the rifle as she did.

Light came from six interlocking circles overhead and on one of the walls was a metal grill. It had been plastered over with iron bars, welded into place. Now the bars were bulging outwards with the pressure of something behind. One by one the bars snapped. A shower of thick, red globs splattered into the room.

2 Battling the jel

Yoona had one hand on the rifle grip; the other flicked over the controls, when a thin streak of burning white light squirted out like water from a hose. The red drops were hovering in the air. They turned black and frizzled like frying bacon. But a thick spout of solid muddy-red followed and moved like a huge, square snake.

'The stairs!' she yelled and pushed hard.

I stumbled towards them and she ducked ahead, stamping her foot hard on a button. A hatch slid open in the ceiling and Yoona gave me another hard push. Up the stairs we went, Yoona behind me. The muddy-red snake was pouring out of the broken grill, heading for us. Yoona fired another jet of laser and it made a high, horrible screaming sound. Then she dragged me through on to the next floor.

A boy was there. The name BREN was black-lettered over his pocket. He had the same type of gun, a brown-red sharp face and dark red hair in two dreadlocks. He swung his laser rifle up and blazed down at the faceless red thing slithering up the steps after us. It screamed again with a thick smell of burning. Yoona stamped on the deck button and the hatch slid back over. A sudden silence, and I was on the upper deck of Deepwater.

'Upper deck' – or the bridge of a ship, whatever you wanted to call it. The deck slanted out lengthways to a rounded point. There were four black metal chairs and a bank of controls studded with twinkling crystals. A wide, curved computer screen was set over a thick window that

9

was shaped like two eyes looking out into darkness.

A girl sat at one of the chairs. Something like a crazy star pattern flickered over her controls. She turned. Silver-grey track suit, dark green hair, light green skin and green eyes.

'Hurry!' she pointed. 'The solunk is just ahead!'

'Positions!' snapped Yoona.

Bren ran for his chair and Yoona pushed me into the one beside her. I was Robbie Mikkelson – no, Reb; a fresh memory seemed to splash over my mind like water on rocks. I sat down in the chair and looked ahead.

Once I had gone on a hydrofoil. You get the feeling of standing still as the boat speeds over the blue water and blue sky stands still overhead. It was like that now. The upper deck of Deepwater was solid like that, but the black space seemed to rush by underneath; we were going at mega-speed. Yoona had slipped into the next seat. She nudged me and pointed ahead.

'There.'

Ahead through the window was black space. And far ahead was a huge lump that glistened like a black iceberg with funny glowing lines on it, like it had been torn out of something blacker. It grew bigger and bigger like a black mountain.

'Stress six,' said the green-haired girl. The name stencilled over her pocket was GRET.

'Stress six field,' repeated Yoona. 'That'll crush Deepwater like a squeeze bottle.' She looked at me, her voice careful but urgent. 'Reb, we hit that thing in less than a minute.'

They looked at me as though I knew what to do. I was blank, and my face showed it. There was a flicker in Yoona's eyes as she realised; real trouble, said her expression. Gret understood too and moaned.

'He's still prexing, we're wiped!'

Yoona took my hand. 'Reb, ask me the entry factor, ask me!'

'What's the entry factor?' I said, looking at that horrible black nothing rushing at us.

'Two point four,' she returned, 'shallow reading.'

'All right, angle two point one.' Was that me? I'd just made a decision to send a spaceship into that thing! I didn't know what I'd said and I was still talking. 'Maximum speed or the sides will whiplash us.'

Yoona had no doubts. Her hand stabbed at the controls and the spaceship trembled slightly. The solunk was filling our screen. I had doubts, though. Something tingled under my tongue and the same voice yelled out of me.

'Two point *two*, two point *two*!'

And it was my hand stabbing the crystals and Deepwater shuddered again, turning a little. It was like getting ready to bash into someone with your shoulder. The solunk charged up and seemed to crash against us like a black wall. The whole spaceship shook with a loud crunching, grinding sound and huge chunks of something bashed against the hull. Then suddenly we were back in clear space.

There was complete silence, then Bren sighed. 'We've been getting too many of these things lately. And they're all different.' He glanced at me and tugged one of his dreadlocks. 'Lucky we've still got you, Reb.' He made it sound like I'd nearly fallen overboard.

'Lucky he re-angled before it was too late,' said Gret. She bent over her star chart without looking at me.

Yoona's mouth smiled a little. She reached under her seat and threw me a squeeze bottle. I know how to use that, too, without being told. Hold it up to the mouth and press the ribbed base very slightly. Result, a cool, thin stream of juice that tastes incredible and is only supercharged water, hits the mouth. There was a heavy thumping sound and everybody snapped back to reality.

'Now the jel,' said Yoona. She spoke into her console again. 'COL, I want a grid readout.'

It flickered up on the huge, curved computer screen over the window. It was a three-dimensional computer graphic of the spaceship these kids called 'Deepwater'.

It was big. *Big*! Like an oblong block with a slightly blunted

11

end, that was us. And size! Imagine passenger jets stacked end to end, imagine a whole ocean liner. Deepwater was very, very big and long.

It was in three sections. The end section was blank, the second had one word, 'NUN', and we were in the front section. It was split up into compartments and criss-cross lines that were ventilation shafts. All the front section, except our deck, was flooded with a deep red.

'That's all jel?' asked Bren. There was fear in his voice. 'It's never got so far, so quickly.'

'It'll burst up here any minute,' said Gret. She tensed in horror.

'No, it won't.' Yoona spoke into the controls again. 'COL, seal off the main deck.'

'Don't forget about us up here,' squeaked an anxious intercom voice.

'You're sealed, Lis.' Yoona smiled faintly. 'COL, open all access below main deck, open airlock and both main ports.'

The main console flashed red. A deep, bored machine-voice said, 'Access opened, airlocks and main port opened.'

Two black circles had appeared on either side of the forward part of the grid pattern. As they did, I seemed to feel the ship slowing down although there was no real sense of movement. I could just feel it, in me. The red began to melt away from the front grid section.

'COL, port-side airlock.'

Up on screen came a close picture of the big, round lock. It was sliding open and a mass of brown-red jelly was being sucked out like a thick rope of spaghetti.

'COL, close when the reading is clear,' said Yoona.

'What's COL?' I asked innocently. Gret hissed sharply like a cat and Yoona shot me a concerned glance.

'Control Operational Link, our systems computer, Reb.'

You *know* this, said her look. 'Voice-activated to you and me.'

'Yoona, he's prexing, you must give Bren voice-ac control,'

12

said Gret. Bren pursed his lips like he was whistling and said nothing. Yoona shook her head and stood up.

I sat there. Once I'd seen a very bad traffic accident and I had that same feeling now – that something was happening all round me and I was not able to stop it or do anything to help.

And it was a hundred times worse to have the really scary feeling that this was OK, that it *should* be happening. That me, Robbie Milkybar-Mikkelson, fourteen years old, was in the middle of the worst and weirdest sci-fi trip ever – and that I wasn't dreaming.

Yoona touched my arm again. 'Up top might clear your head.'

Up top? I stood up and Yoona's firm hand pushed me right round to face a small spiral stairway set against the rear wall. Bren and Gret were whispering together. I walked over and went up the stairs, Yoona close behind me. We went through a deck opening and I gasped because it was like stepping on to the top of the spaceship in outer space.

'Up top' was a thick glass bubble set over the control deck. The glass was so clear I could almost reach out and touch the twinkling black mass of deep space. Behind it the length of the spaceship stretched away, ridged in the centre like a backbone, plated with a dark grey-silver, like fish-scales. And on either side, outside the bubble, two long tubes like battleship cannon pointed into the darkness. Two more strange-coloured kids in the silver-grey track suits were there.

'Zak and Lis,' whispered Yoona from behind.

A boy was standing, watching the streaks of jel disappear behind the spaceship. He had a golden-yellow skin and black hair streaked with orange and blue. He looked over and waved with a tired smile.

In the centre, lying on a big, double recliner chair, was a girl.

She had pale blue skin and deep blue hair, yellowed at the ends. Her face was chubby and she had big yellow eyes like a cat. The black stencil-letters over her pocket spelled LIS.

13

There were two binocular-like viewers over the chair and she was holding on to one of them with handles at the side. Both had long tubes that went up through the bubble roof between the cannon-tubes. Like the others she looked really dead, but she grinned.

'Hi, Reb, take a turn on lookout?' Even as she spoke, she never stopped spinning the recliner around, moving the viewing scope up and down, always alert.

'He's still prexing,' said Yoona.

Lis stopped her chair. The boy, Zak, turned. Both had the same look on their faces, the way Dad looked when his job was chopped.

'You'll get over it,' said Lis. It was the way Dad talked – he was *sure* he'd get another job. 'You busted that last solunk all right.'

'Did I?' It seemed the most honest thing to say.

Zak darted another look at me. He opened then shut his mouth. Lis began to swivel her chair again, but both had the same expression on their faces. Fear.

'You do know you're on Deepwater?' said Zak.

'I know this is a spaceship.' I went on being honest. 'But I live in a house with my parents and Earth hasn't got real space travel yet.'

'Earth!' gasped Lis. Her chair jerked again but did not stop.

Zak looked at me rigidly. 'You do know what trites are?' he said, like a teacher *knowing* you haven't got the answer.

Yoona answered for me. 'Reb doesn't know anything,' she said. 'He was still prexing when that strip showed up. The jel was nearly on top of us, too, so I boosted him back.'

Silence. They really felt that. Zak turned away and Lis's movements on the recliner were as jerky as a wind-up toy, like she wasn't thinking about it at all. Yoona went on, carefully, taking all the blame. 'It was my decision. We needed him for the solunk.'

'He'll snap out of it, though, won't he?' Lis held tight on to the hand-grips, her face up close to the scope. Her voice was

14

muffled and broke a little. 'We always snap out of it.'

'Yes, he broke us out of that solunk,' said Zak. 'He must know who he is.' He. They weren't talking about Reb any more – just 'he'.

'Instinct,' said Yoona. 'We can't rely on that.'

Lis jerked her chair round again. 'Can Gret take over now?' she asked. 'I've really had it.'

She wouldn't look at me and neither would Zak. It was like the time I missed a main school match and we lost. There's nothing you can say to the rest of the team – you've let them down and never mind how good the excuse was. Yoona touched my arm again and led the way back down to the main deck.

What the hell was happening?

3 The dream people

When we got down, Bren and Gret were still whispering. They didn't look round. Ahead of them, outside the slanting windows, were the black, sparkling fields of space. I was standing on the deck of a spaceship, and it was still totally unreal.

'What's that?' I pointed to the far distance ahead. A thin red and yellow line divided the blackness like a sunset.

'Nebula,' said Yoona shortly. She was looking at the on-screen grid pattern. All the red was gone now. 'COL, seal ship.' The black circles began to disappear.

Yoona waited until it was gone. 'Gret, go and relieve Lis,' she said. 'I'm below deck, briefing Reb.'

'There's another meteor shoal ahead.' Bren tugged a dreadlock as he spoke. 'Trites love asteroids. Good cover.'

'We'll go round it,' said Yoona flatly.

Gret stood up and folded her arms. 'What if the trites hit us while you're briefing him?' Him, like I didn't exist. Her green eyes flashed. 'You have to give Bren voice-access to COL!'

'I'll decide that.' Yoona's yellow-brown eyes went hard as diamonds. She stamped her foot on a deck button and the hatch slid open. 'Now do as you're told.'

Gret hesitated, then headed for the stairs with a sulky look. Bren whistled mockingly and pulled his dreadlock again. Yoona motioned me below and the hatch closed over.

Below, the scorch-marks of her laser still criss-crossed the walls. All the jel had gone. The walls weren't even sticky, but there was a strange, sickly smell in the air. Yoona spoke sharply.

'COL, ventilate.'

Something hissed for a moment and the smell went. She pushed me in front of a narrow mirror panel by the bunk and pointed. 'Reb, that is *you*.'

My face was golden brown, with a different, tense look. My hair was down to my shoulders, the same black with a broad streak of blue-red down one side. I had one earring on, a small thick hoop of red plastic. But my face, my eyes and my voice were the same.

'I'm Robbie Mikkelson, I don't know your Reb.'

'Get in the lick, freshen up,' she snapped. She was glaring, very frustrated.

'What's a lick?'

'Shower!' She pushed me to a narrow door set in the wall, opened it and shoved me in.

It must have been automatic. Several blasts of water and hot air hit me from all sides. I was wet and dry in ten seconds, like being licked by a giant cat's tongue. Yoona dragged me out and pushed me in front of the mirror again.

'Reb, that's *you*, now snap out of it!' I just looked at her and thought for a moment she was going to hit me. She yelled, 'Reb, you are a South Martian, south-west quadrant of Araxes. You were born there and have never been to Earth. You were on Mars, then on this spaceship.'

'How did we get here?'

'I don't know!' She was yelling again. 'But we're from the solar colonies and now we're on this spaceship!' She gave a quick gasp. 'That's all any of us know, Reb.'

I swallowed. 'I don't even know that. And I'm Robbie Mikkelson. I still don't know your Reb.'

I thought again that she was going to hit me. Then I realised she was very frightened. She gently pushed me down on to a bed and sat opposite. She put her hands over her face and talked through them like Lis with the viewer.

'I boosted you because I didn't dare hit that black, solid chunk of nothing on my own. We would have crushed.' She

18

took her hands away and looked at me. Her eyes were full of tears. 'I'm sorry.'

'Boosted – from my prex . . .' My voice, but the words meant nothing.

Yoona nodded. 'Prexing, pre-existing hallucinations. They come from time to time, but they're bad dreams, they always go.' She ran her hands through her blonde hair and the red streaks tangled in her fingers. 'Until you, Reb.'

'All I can remember is being a schoolkid,' I said. 'I don't know anything about this ship, where I am or if you're the people in a dream.'

'Dream people.' Yoona nearly laughed. 'Reb, *we* are real, the Earth-schoolkid part of you is a dream. That boost somehow zapped your memory and now you think you're someone else – maybe someone from a vid-book on Earth. Don't you remember, NUN taught us all this?'

I shook my head like a dumb, switched-off schoolkid.

'Do you know who NUN is?' she said. Her voice was more guarded.

NUN? That name on the grid readout. I shook my head again. Above, the hatch slid open and Lis came down. She didn't look at Yoona or me, just stumbled over and dropped on to the bunk opposite. She was asleep at once, face down and one arm over the side, like she was knocked out.

Yoona was still watching me. 'Energy rods are knocking on the starboard lower coil,' she said suddenly.

'Re-jig them. COL can stream power from the main coil.' My voice but not my words, just like when we hit the solunk. And like then, a little echo under my tongue.

'You can still respond to problems.' Yoona was thinking hard, puzzled. She stood up. 'Well schoolkid, Reb must be in there somewhere.'

She crossed to Lis and gently rolled the sleeping girl over into the centre of the bunk. Lis did not wake. Yoona came back and stood watching me for a moment. Then she sighed.

'Get some rest.'

19

Zak came down the steps with a toolkit. He didn't look at either of us, but crossed over and began to repair the grill. Yoona was about to go up the stairs, then came back to me. Her voice dropped to a whisper.

'Schoolkid, if you do find Reb, send him back first. I need him.' She went back up the stairs. The hatch closed. Silence.

'I', not 'we', she had said. I had a sense she was expecting trouble. The air still had a faintly sickly smell and Zak's welder hissed. I looked round.

Everything in the room was metal and grey. There was nothing about kids here, no posters, clothes, gear chucked about all over the floor. Not even blankets on the beds. Each had a metal locker clipped to the end. That was all.

There were two doors at either end with big metal lettering, AIRLOCK ENTRY, stamped over them. The stairs to the upper deck were in the middle, and opposite them was another door, set deeply into the wall and shaped to a point. Something made me get up and look at it.

It was narrow and made of metal like everything else. Etched over it was a large circle with a small V-shaped nick at the top. Inside was a set of strange symbols, also cut into the metal. Behind me, Zak's welder had stopped hissing and I could feel his eyes upon me.

The symbols and circle didn't mean anything, but this was the door Yoona looked at when she talked about NUN. NUN? Something else that didn't make sense.

'You couldn't forget NUN,' said Zak from behind me. His voice had a tense high sound to it. 'No matter how bad the prex.'

I didn't reply. I just walked over to my bed and sat down. I had a feeling that to say anything would just make things more difficult for Yoona. Without meaning to, I nodded.

'We should all be back with NUN. I still think NUN is just cross with us because we wanted too much.' His voice was wistful now, like remembering a magic holiday. 'But just for a time; we'll get back.' I said nothing and a moment later the welder began to hiss again.

I sat on my bed and shut my eyes a moment. My head spun like a blender.

Nothing made sense. There were two people inside me and one of them wasn't real. I was scared because I didn't know who I was. And because I was here, on a huge, long spaceship in outer space. Weird.

I lay back on the bed. The welder hissed and hissed. In my head, the blender spun round and round. Everything went dizzy and black and the darkness only stopped spinning when a loud voice woke me up.

'Breakfast, son, get it or forget it.'

I sat up in bed, blinking. I was in pyjamas and Dad was at the door. I looked at my bedside clock. Nine o'clock! I went straight into a survival mode.

'Dad, I'll need a note for Ms Booth.'

'Not unless school's on Saturday.' He grinned and went.

Saturday. Yes, yesterday was Friday so my crazy dream was . . . last night? But I couldn't remember last night. I got dressed slowly. My jeans and T-shirt felt wrong, like they should have been a silver-grey track suit. I didn't tell Dad what had happened and I wasn't hungry.

He went on his lawnmowing round. David was hacking all weekend with his mad computer mates and Sarah was doing ballet. Mum wouldn't be back from the supermarket until late afternoon. I needed to be on my own. I needed sunshine, sitting still and hard thinking, because the dream memory wouldn't go away. Of kids with yellow, blue and green hair. The jel and its horrible smell. Thinking about what trites were – or NUN. A spaceship so real I could still feel it moving round me.

The sun was very hot. All that brightness seemed strange, as though I'd spent my life away from it. So I went into my bedroom and sat down. I looked all around and waited. No Yoona. Maybe she had her hands full with Bren and Gret – a real pair of troublemakers, those two. Even Ms Booth would have had problems sorting them out.

21

I shut my eyes in a long, tight squeeze, then opened them. Everything was still there. The poster from the pop concert, the stealth bomber hanging from the ceiling, my clothes chucked everywhere. And, just for a second, it seemed more unreal that that metal below-deck room on Deepwater.

I was very scared and the feeling grew worse. I wanted to sleep, but one half of me was afraid of waking up on Deepwater. The other half said go for it.

I shouldn't be tired. Dad said I'd snored like a pig all night. But I was. I got Mum's alarm clock and set it for noon. I could sleep and the alarm would wake me in two hours in case the jel was eating me. Or those other things – trites. Not funny, kiddo, I said aloud, then lay back and closed my eyes.

The bed was very comfortable. Everything was nice, dark and peaceful and the clock ticked loudly beside me. I remember turning over and the clock somehow stopped ticking. Then the alarm went off. Not the usual bell-sound, but a horrible loud screaming like a maniac chainsaw. I sat up and, opposite me, Lis jerked upright.

'Reb, move!' she yelled.

She was off her bed, running for the door. She grabbed my wrist and pulled me along, yelling again.

'Trites!'

22

4 Trite fight

The hatch slid open and the alarm stopped as we ran up on to the deck. I had a moment to realise that none of this seemed quite so strange. Bren and Yoona were in the control chairs. Yoona turned.

'Trites, where?' gasped Lis, clutching her blue hair and looking round, still half asleep.

'False alarm, sorry,' said Yoona.

The thin red-yellow stripe of nebula was much closer and over to the left. It was like a broad ribbon trailing long, straggly ends.

'Zak thought he saw them in the nebula,' said Bren.

'If Zak said he saw them, then he saw them,' snapped Lis.

Bren grinned and pulled a deep red dreadlock. And stuff you too, it meant.

'We did an all-point scan,' said Yoona. She looked at me, about to ask a question.

'A scan won't help if the nebulae are radioactive,' I heard myself saying. Yes, me. 'The trites will be blocked.' Lis yelped and was off, running up the stairs.

'Trites aren't smart enough for that,' said Bren uncertainly.

'Yes they are,' said my voice again. Yoona was looking at me like she didn't dare hope.

'Relieve Gret,' she said. I didn't have to. Gret came clattering down the stairs, furious because Lis had pulled her away from the viewers. 'Go on, Reb,' said Yoona. 'We can handle Deepwater.'

I went. Something inside me said the trites were close. As I did, I heard Gret's sour-apples voice, 'Yoona, thirty-six hours, you're going to total out.'

Upstairs, Zak and Lis were in the recliner, on a viewer each, and spinning round, clutching tight to the handles. Zak looked over and they stopped spinning for a moment.

'Nothing,' he said. 'Want a look?'

Zak got up. I hesitated, then lowered myself down. I was still Robbie, but the little Reb-echo inside me knew enough to find the viewing sights, set the hand-grips and foot-pedals. Lis flipped a strap over my body, but I left it. The spaceship gravity was just like being on Earth.

'Hey, strap in,' she said. 'If Yoona starts chucking Deepwater around to avoid trites, you'll bounce all over the bubble.' She seemed concerned I'd forgotten something so obvious. I saw the look she and Zak exchanged. They just weren't sure about this kid.

'Do you want fire control?' she asked.

'Ah . . . no thanks.'

No way. I was a schoolkid and I didn't even know what a trite *was*. I took a firm hold and pressed my eyes to the viewing scope.

It was like sitting in a huge cinema screen that went all round the theatre. The viewer was like a cat's eye, lighting up the black so that stars and nebulae were much more clear and sharp.

I touched a ridge of controls by the hand-grip and a 'star' magnified up in its own tight video frame, a whirling chunk of cratered rock. Another press and it zapped back into place. I began to move the scope and the all-round cinema screen spun with me. Beside me, Lis spoke softly.

'You do the nebula, I'll do topside.'

Two viewers covered the horizon like a pair of eyes. The nebula close-up was red and orange, split out at the ends into long, yellow strips. The screen misted and flickered with the radiation.

'See anything?' asked Lis.

24

'No.'

See *what*? You are still Robbie, I yelled to me, you don't even know what a trite is. Then I did know what a trite was. Because the ribbon strands of nebula flicked open and they came out, like streaks of light, straight for Deepwater.

'Trites!' My voice, Reb's words. 'Bearing M-6, Quadrant Three!'

The screen snapped as Lis locked on-line and ran the gunsight over. The trites were already halfway across and the decks jarred as she fired the laser cannon. Her hand must have been very close to the fire controls.

Eight of them. They were like boomerangs with upturned wingtips and quickly as they moved, Lis was quicker. She zapped four with four strikes. They split up and the turret spun, Lis locking the gunsights and blasting one more. But those nebulae were too close and three got through, darting with incredible speed through the laser fire to reach Deepwater.

'Three are down,' Zak yelled and over the intercom came Yoona's calm 'responding' as the trites landed just where our laser cannon couldn't reach – overhead on top of the bubble, between the cannon.

We were looking directly up at them. They skidded a moment, then each one grew four thin, spiky legs and spread beetle wings to keep balance. Two eyes grew out on stalks and looked down at us like we were hamburgers.

The spaceship shook round us and squeeze-bottles clattered through the turret. The star horizon altered as Yoona jerked Deepwater upward to try and shake the trites loose into laser fire. One did spin up outside the cannon and Lis melted it with a dazzling burst.

The last two skidded, but grew another four legs each and hung on like horrible spiders. A long sharp sting grew out of each belly. No, not a sting, a drill. They were drilling in!

Lis gasped in pure terror. 'If they crack the iron-glass, we're finished!'

Zak was clinging to the stairwell, legs locked round the rail.

The angle jerked again as Yoona stood Deepwater on end. But the trites hung on and their drill-stings began to turn. Tiny bits of iron-glass were flying already and, for a moment, I froze helpless. Then Reb's awareness seemed to punch me like a fist.

'Yoona, tell COL the gun-turret bearings are too hot. Flood them!' That was *me* talking about the rotation-gear that turns the guns inside the turret – things I didn't know about!

'Hey!' yelled Lis.

Yoona didn't hesitate. I heard her shout on the intercom. 'COL, flood gun-turret bearings.'

'Turret bearings are stable.' COL's voice was flat and smug like a teacher crushing us with facts. More glass flew – the trites were gripping tight and drilling hard. I grabbed the centre crystal – somehow I knew which one it was and held it with all my strength.

I could feel COL's power trying to turn the crystal. Lis must have realised what I was doing, for she pressed her hand hard over mind. Even then, that wasn't enough and Yoona shouted again.

'COL, the bearing is jammed. This is a command, flood it!'

Bits of iron-glass were flying as the trites drilled. Then the gun-bearings hummed loudly round us and streaks of fluid flooded over the bubble in sticky yellow patches.

One of the trites slipped and fell off. Lis zapped it at once. The other hung on and drilled. Deepwater jerked again and the nebula-horizon turned upside-down as Yoona took the whole bulk of the spaceship over. We were held by our seat-belts and Zak by his grip on the railings.

The other trite drilled a moment longer, then lost its footing. It hung for a moment by its drill-sting, but was swept back into space. It recovered, but Lis flashed the laser a last time. The trite melted and vanished.

There were two small drill-craters overhead in the dome. I would later find out that this was the closest trites had come to getting in. The squeeze-bottles clattered again and the nebula-horizon moved with Deepwater as Yoona turned the spaceship round and upright in a slow circle. Although a mega-long spaceship, she was handling it like a skateboard. The nebula fell behind and space closed around – deep space with colour-splashes as though somebody had emptied paint-pots into black water, all different colours, shapes and movement jiggling together.

'Come down, Reb,' said Yoona over the intercom. Zak was untangling himself from the rail and shakily standing upright.

'Go on,' said Lis. Her hand squeezed mine in thanks. 'We can handle things now.' She looked pale as death but gave a cheeky grin. 'You go and wreck something else for COL.'

Zak was rubbing his legs. He tried to smile too, but as I went down the stairs I heard him say, 'We won't fool COL like that again. The trites nearly got us that time.'

I kept going down the stairs. That was just the problem. They didn't have Reb back. Sure, he was inside me while the trites attacked, like a hand in a boxing-glove. But I was still Robbie. And I was calling it quits.

I was sick, weak at the knees and breathless, my body hurting from the tight straps. This nightmare had gone on too long. It was time to tell Yoona and the others, then wait for Mum's alarm to snap me out of this weird dream once and for all. Because that was all it was, that was all it *could* be. Time to go home.

Below, the three of them were unstrapping themselves. Yoona said, 'COL, automatic,' and stood up. 'Good work.' She gave that little smile.

'Yeah, good work, Reb,' said Bren. He nearly smiled.

'Or is it still Robbie the Earthkid?' Gret didn't smile.

This was it, and I was going to tell them. I think Yoona guessed it because she walked over and cut in, a bit too quickly. 'Reb, take over control, I have to sleep.'

She was standing in front of me. Her hand gripped my wrist and squeezed it tight – a long, silent scream for help. Yoona had done thirty-six hours' duty, then thrown Deepwater round

27

like a skateboard. She was at the very end of her strength and nobody was allowed to see it but me.

'All right,' I said. It was so crazy that I didn't dare stop and think. And Yoona was too tired even to smile. She slipped something hard and round like a coin into my hand and turned a moment.

'Bren, relieve Zak,' and slightly louder, 'COL, control is with Reb, repeat, control is with Reb.' She walked on past and down the stairs. The deck hatch closed.

Bren and Gret looked at me. I didn't look back. It was like acting in the school play. I walked over and sat down. As I did, my red earring crackled sharply and Yoona's voice buzzed in my ear.

'We're on pilot intercom. COL is the centre console and it'll glow red to show it understands.' Her voice was quick, jerky and stumbled. 'I must sleep. Look after Deepwater, please? I'll explain everything later. Please, Robbie – the journal disc is voice-activated . . .'

She stopped speaking. I think she just fainted. 'Robbie' – she knew I wasn't her co-pilot but she needed me. I was Reb when the trites attacked, so I had to be Reb again. And I had a fair idea that Reb didn't like Gret or Bren.

'Bren, you heard Yoona,' I said.

I didn't look at him. There was a long moment before I heard his footsteps go slowly over to the stairs. I waited a moment longer for Gret to sit down, but she didn't.

'You can't fool me,' she said. 'You're still prexing.'

There was just enough of an uncertain edge for me to ignore her. But Gret wasn't that easily put off.

'What's my duty?' she said.

I remembered the star chart hologram flickering over her controls. 'Course navigation,' I said. Silence from Gret. Lucky guess!

Zak came down the stairs, stamped on the deck button and went below. Gret was still looking at me.

'All right then, Reb,' she said in a very silky-smooth way.

'You're not the Earthkid any more, you're co-pilot to our brave, bold Yoona. So . . . no more prexing?'

I waited. I knew that tone from teachers, parents and adults in general. When they were laying verbal traps, they always do it with sarcasm.

'So tell me, Reb,' said Gret, 'what is our destination? And how long before we get there?'

Warning. When we hit the solunk (I still didn't know what a solunk was), and when the trites hit us (and I still didn't know what they were), I had spoken like Reb without meaning to. Then, there was a funny little echo at the back of my tongue, just under the sound of me speaking, like static. It was as though pressure had locked me on to a new wave-length.

I was pressured *now*. I felt that little echo tickle in my mouth. So I spoke, because waiting a moment would be too long – Gret was too sharp. Three words slipped out too easily and scared the hell out of me.

'Nowhere,' I said. 'Destination unknown.'

Gret looked at me, then bent over her controls. Her long, dark green hair fell round her face. And what I said sank in with me, too.

I wasn't Robbie the schoolkid any more. No way was all this a freaky dream. I opened my hand on the hard round thing that Yoona had slipped me. A journal disc, she called it.

Did she think there were answers for me there? About what had happened to me? How I had somehow changed places with Reb and was co-pilot on a super-giant spaceship – somewhere in the galaxy and going nowhere we knew about?

Because I was here now. I'd made that decision because she needed me. And unless I pre-existed again, then I would stay here.

Then I remembered Mum's alarm clock.

5 In the beginning

I don't know how long I sat there. It was very strange because I still didn't know if I was inside Reb – or if he was inside me. Gret didn't bother me again, but my stomach knotted like a wet towel when I thought about what was happening. I had to make myself relax or I would just fall apart.

Deepwater did that for me. The movement of the spaceship was so gentle and everything outside so incredible that I did relax. I even forgot Mum's alarm clock was supposed to be ticking somewhere. It was just the magic of being at the controls of a spaceship because outside, outer space was so beautiful.

Every picture I'd seen of it showed mostly black, but it was full of bright and dark colours – a lot of black, but big misty sunflowers of red and yellow that were nebulae clouds. Also long see-through swirls and curtains of dark purple mist – traces of long-ago explosions, I supposed. Once I saw a solid mass of green and orange gas that the spaceship went sideways round, very carefully, and a tangled mass of long blue ribbons that went on and on into the blackness.

And Deepwater was so easy to fly when there were no trites around to avoid. COL made all the minor course corrections and always announced them first.

'COL to pilot, variant twelve, meteoroid.'

'COL, confirmed.' Reb must have said that dozens of times but I had to swallow a tickle in my throat. I didn't look at Gret. Deepwater made a very slight inclination and a small cratered lump of space rock rumbled past below us. A digital readout flickered as it did. The 'small chunk' was house-sized, solid iron-ore and weighed several hundred thousand kilos.

Some of the nebulae were like long thin veils and once a whole shower of meteors passed above, sparkling with starlight like huge diamonds, also as big as houses. Then an orange sheen of mist and again Deepwater tilted, going up and over. Gret's readout said it was harmless, but COL never took chances and never let Deepwater touch anything. Whoever programmed COL had done a careful and thorough job.

I felt a little tingle of panic. Mum's alarm clock was ticking somewhere and suddenly I became aware that a lot of time had slipped by. I still needed answers. Gret seemed asleep, so I lifted the journal disc to my lips. Voice-activated, Yoona had said.

'Where are we?' I asked.

'Position unknown.' Yoona's voice buzzed in my earring communicator, the words clipped, sentences patched together from the ship's memory banks. 'I have asked COL – no answer. Past all island galaxies, known star positions, we call this Colour-space, function of most colour-formations unknown. Gulfs of deep black space between them, we time-blink over these.' I squeezed the edges of the disc and the voice stopped.

Colour-space? Time-blinking? Now there were big, important questions pressuring inside me and I couldn't handle them yet. So I asked the little ones.

'What are solunks?'

'Solunks – solid chunks of solar nothing, Reb says – maybe super-hard space distortion, compressed matter – like a sonic iceberg – seeing more of them – too big to go round but hit them right and they break up – getting bigger.'

So Reb called them solunks. Solid chunks of solar nothing – that was neat of me. I whispered again, aware I was running out of easy questions.

'Trites?'

'Space insects, genus unknown. Maybe can store air somehow between planets – like the insects on Mars that can bore into solid rock and lay their eggs in the stone-slugs. Cannot penetrate hull, so attack iron-glass—'

I remembered the hungry look those things had given us. We were the only living things on Deepwater, and they would lay their eggs in us. Time for a big question.

'Prexing.'

'Prexing, pre-existing, dream-state of another life before this.' Yoona's voice was strained; none of them liked talking about prexes. 'We prex back to our lives on the planets we came from. Myself, Reb, Gret and Lis on Mars, Zak the Moon city, Bren on Ceres, mining base for Jupiter. I can use a brain-link to enter a prex—'. Then the last entry, 'Reb has prexed but I found him in a schoolroom on Planet Earth, late twentieth century, something is wrong—'

I stopped the disc. Yes, something was wrong, so she came back and got me. She needed Reb. And they were all supposed to be from planets or moons. But when?

'What are our prexing dates?'

'Myself, Gret, Lis, Reb and Bren, ninth decade, twenty-first century (about a hundred years from now!), Zak about fifty years earlier.'

I stopped. This was getting more and more fantastic. Not just space shuttles and going to the Moon. A hundred years on, the human race had colonised the Moon and Mars, even as far as Jupiter. Prexing was a kind of flashback to a former life, but it still didn't tell me who I was. Maybe nobody knew. I whispered again, one word that had been sitting on my tongue like a solunk.

'NUN.'

'NUN controls most of Deepwater. All we know about NUN is the voice, neither male nor female—'

I stopped the disc again to think, but somehow Yoona's voice carried on.

'We know almost nothing about NUN, but it's looked after us since we can first remember.'

It was Yoona's normal voice. Normal and less tired than before, she even smiled as she sat down beside me. She looked a lot cleaner and more relaxed. I couldn't believe I'd been sitting at the controls for six hours. The time had passed like blinking.

'How long did it take you to ask about NUN?'

'A long time,' I said.

She nodded. The console glowed red under her hand as she took control. She paused, read the flickering digitals and looked out at space.

'I love all this. It's the only life I've known. All of us.'

'Except for prexing,' I said.

'Prexing isn't life.'

'How can—' I broke off.

Yoona looked at me. 'Go on.'

'How can you think this is life? Trying to run this spaceship all the time?'

'It wasn't always like this, Robbie.'

She guided Deepwater round a very small solunk. She was silent for a time. Yoona had thought a lot about NUN, but this was the first time she had to explain it.

'A golden room with a magic cave.'

That was where NUN lived. Yoona began to talk about it. 'The place where our lives began. I remember the darkness first. Then I saw a light. It – it seemed to come on inside my head.'

When Yoona opened her eyes, she explained, she was in a big, big room that was filling with light. Imagine a sports field roofed over like a church and plated floor to ceiling with pure gold. She and the other five were in the very centre, in a row of low beds like our bunks. A crystal cover had just lifted from each one. There were two more of these crystal-cover things, but they did not open.

The room was bare of anything except gold and light. At each end was an arched door, also of that pure golden metal. The circle and symbols on the below-deck door were stamped on these doors, too.

'A golden room with a magic cave,' repeated Yoona softly.

On one side was a deep walk-in terminal, big as the upper

deck of Deepwater itself. It was studded with large crystals like the small ones on the deck controls. Even the floor and ceiling were crystals and they flashed with a million sharp colours.

'We didn't know what anything was for. We didn't even know who we were,' she said.

They were naked. But there were silver-grey track suits at the end of each 'wake-up casket', as they called them. Their names were stencilled over each pocket.

'We got up. We weren't tired, but our legs were a bit weak. We even found talking funny, but we knew how to talk, we knew we were kids, that sort of thing. We were all right. Then we heard the voice.'

The voice. Yoona's eyes were half closed. She wasn't tired. She was remembering the first day of her life when the voice spoke.

'The voice of NUN.'

6 *The golden giver*

The voice of NUN had sounded all round them and came from nowhere. It was the first voice they heard. They bonded to NUN because NUN was the only thing in their lives – father and mother and giver of everything.

'Everything,' said Yoona. 'You have to understand that.'

And I did, because I could almost feel the golden light on my own bare body and hear that wonderful caring voice. Six children were waking up to a wonderful time of happiness where everything was done for them – everything. NUN gave them their food – blue biscuits and water, but NUN could make the biscuits taste of any flavour. And the water, any colour or sparkle they wanted, even where the inset shower rooms and toilets were. Everything they needed was in the NUN super-room.

And the 'magic-cave' terminal created anything. NUN made clothes for them, any fashion they liked, from the Stone Age upward to the solar colonies. They could dress like an Egyptian pharoah, a medieval knight, Victorian, punk, Martian shuttle-jockey or worm-hunter. Or mix them all together. NUN showed all this and made them anything they wanted.

Things, too. NUN just projected a hologram screen to show all of Earth's history up to the twenty-first century and solar exploration. They only had to ask for something; the terminal would flash and it was there, a Roman statue or a virtual reality helmet, a light-music system, an asteroid rock-skimmer or a Jupiter moonstone.

'I think even before NUN taught us, we had a subconscious memory of the colonies,' said Yoona. 'Life was always tough there and plain, so we chose bright and beautiful things.'

They hung the walls and covered the floor with anything that looked interesting. Persian carpets, red glitter-sand from Io (one of Jupiter's moons), black crystals from the asteroid belt, silks from Earth or the Martian rainbow-bug.

They were allowed one animal pet each. Not real ones, of course, but NUN's 'solid-holograms' looked, sounded and even smelled like the real thing, though they didn't need food. They were also life-size, so Zak didn't get his first dinosaur choice (a Tyrannosaurus about six metres high!), and for the same reason, Gret didn't get her leopard.

'Bren got an android-monkey and Lis asked for a Martian sand-diver, one leg, big ears, long tail and all.' Yoona smiled. 'I asked for a parrot.'

She was silent, watching the blackness outside and a cloud of red dots in the distance, caught in the dream of her own memories.

'We'd only read about planet Earth in vid-books, so it was magic making some of the history. My parrot could speak.' She smiled sadly, thinking about her parrot. Now a shoal of glittery meteors like diamond dust was drifting by.

'COL, starboard variant three.'

COL altered course and took Deepwater to one side. Yoona spoke softly again and a huge pair of blades like windscreen-wipers moved once over the eye-windows. Never go near anything, never take chances – that was how she flew her spaceship.

Those first months in the NUN room were an inter-galactic 21st-century Disneyland, a holiday that never ended. Then NUN the giver became NUN the teacher, telling them about Earth and the solar colonies they came from. Some areas were blocked. They could not learn anything after the year 2150. It was enough to know about the settlements on Mars – how their skin and hair tints were the result of early 'terraforming' (whatever that meant), that changed ozone-layers, and the protective filters on their glassed-in 'py-sets'. And about Earth, suffocating in the stink of its own pollution. But nothing about families or homes. Their direct link was always with NUN.

Yoona was the first to ask questions – why they were there and what was happening; why they were living their lives in this room and how long they would be here. NUN simply didn't answer those questions, or about why two of the wake-up caskets stayed closed.

Then at the end of one learning period, the lights dimmed and they went to their beds. Yoona had a sense that something was wrong – it was in the air, in the way NUN spoke. And that night she had a dream that one of the closed doors was opening, that all of them were running in a terrible panic.

'When we woke, we thought we were dreaming. But it was real.'

They were in another room, what they knew now as their below deck area. It was grey metal and they were lying on narrow hard bunks, clad in their silver-grey track suits. They were totally closed in. The airlock door and the NUN door would not open. A flight of metal steps led up to the ceiling and stopped.

'At first we thought it was some kind of test, or even a hologram that had gone wrong. Then when NUN stayed away and was silent, the others blamed me for asking all those questions. They said I'd offended NUN.'

She guided Deepwater in another upward curve over the long yellow string of a comet tail.

'I felt it was more than punishment. We were here to do something.'

So Yoona didn't waste time bashing the NUN door to try and make it open. She found the food and water machines, and toolkits, medical locker, even more showers and toilets. She started thinking while the others were still in shock. And she soon realised why the only stairway in the room ended at the ceiling.

Because the 'ceiling' was an entrance to another deck. She pressed the right button and the hatch slid open. So

39

they went through . . . and found out for the first time where they were.

On a spaceship. Alone.

'We all got a bit freaked out then, Robbie. Even me.'

They were alone on a spaceship moving through the middle of a strange nowhere. There was no sign of any other crew and they were cut off from the only life-support they knew. Their golden-voiced protector had gone. Yes, they would all get a bit upset about that. Even Yoona.

The only sign of another crew member was one glove on the deck by the main console. Yoona took it from under her seat and showed it to me. The letter 'K' was stencilled on the wrist-part. It was too big when I slipped it on – adult size. But whoever left it had gone without trace.

'Then COL announced itself and we took over running the spaceship,' Yoona said.

Just like that, they took over running the spaceship. COL was a voice-activated control system and it told them everything about the ship except where it was going. Power came from solar energy coils that also somehow created an artificial gravity so they could move OK without floating around. They used the crystals for basic control and COL's voice-ac for the major movement and speed.

'We were scared at first. Then it wore off because we somehow got a feeling from inside . . . like programming . . . that all this was meant to happen.'

But running the spaceship wasn't that easy. Jel was the first problem and Yoona couldn't keep the loathing from her voice when she talked about it. The disgust and fear. Because they all hated jel.

It was brown-red Plasticine-type stuff that surged out of the lower deck ventilation shaft soon after they took control. Zak put his hand on it and nearly stripped the skin off. So they made laser welding torches into rifles and went armed at all times. They learned how to blow it out of the airlocks, but it always somehow remade itself and came back, as horrible as

40

ever. So they cleaned out the vent shafts at regular intervals and that seemed to keep it down.

At first the voyage was easy. COL did most of the work and they had time to relax and learn their duties. COL responded to Yoona's voice, so she became captain. She voice-linked Reb as second in command. He was dependable, she said (meaning me), and spent all his time finding out more and more about the spaceship.

Bren and Gret did most of the forward scanning and navigation to take them round the worst meteor shoals and even stray comets. Lis and Zak manned the turret laser to blast away magnetic meteors, 'mag-mets', that always headed straight for them.

'It all seemed easy. We almost began to feel normal again. Then the prexing started.'

Lis was the first. She had gone into a sudden deep faint like a coma. The medical equipment on the ship was, like everything else, easy to use, practical. Yoona tried a brain-link, like a doctor's stethoscope but a million times more hi-tech. It worked as it did with me.

'It was like getting into someone's dreams, like standing in their brains,' she said.

There were four 'Sets' on Mars. Lis prexed to somewhere called Cydonia in the north-west quadrant, a tough little place, part of an extended family. She was training to be a technician to control robot-probes in the asteroid belt. Then Zak prexed, to the Moon city where he got caught up in some kind of landing accident. Then Gret, also to Mars, to Syrtis in the north-east quadrant, her parents killed by a meteor strike. Bren was born on Ceres, the largest asteroid in the belt and base for Jupiter's moons. He had already mined on two of them. All the 'Jupies' were a bit crazy, Yoona said.

None of the prexes made sense. They were ordinary solar colony kids, all caught up in an accident, doing adult work. But kids grew up fast in those places.

'I suppose the others are a bit scared of me.' Yoona frowned

41

– she didn't like that. 'I went into their prexes, so I know a lot about them. Maybe more than I should. And they know nothing about me.'

'Why not?' I asked.

'I haven't prexed,' said Yoona. Her hand went into a tight fist. 'Not yet, anyway.'

That was something else to annoy Gret and Bren. They came from different quadrants to Yoona and didn't want her in charge. Bren thought he should be second-in-command and Gret was always stirring to get him voice-ac to COL.

'Zak and Lis?'

Yoona smiled again. 'Lis doesn't bother with anything so long as she can blast one mag-met a day. Zak's a lot more moody; the Moon city was always a halfway world, no proper sunlight or anything. He wants NUN back more than any of us.'

And then Deepwater was entering Colour-space and suddenly there was real danger outside. They'd all thought of deep space as somewhere empty and black, but Colour-space was nothing like that. It was full of unknown and terrible danger.

It was a jungle of alien monsters.

7   Monsters of space

At first it was just adventures: the giant asteroid that wasn't one, the something that was either an alien spacecraft or a huge space insect. The nebula whirlpool and what happened when Deepwater nearly went through the tail of a blue comet.

Then the first solunks. They were small and could be avoided. Then bigger, and Reb learned how to nudge them with the bulk of Deepwater. Now they were bigger still and because their forcefield pulled Deepwater in, they had to be rammed at full speed.

'Then the trites hit us,' Yoona related. The first time was nearly the last. A flock of the horrible things zoomed out of nowhere and attacked Deepwater with their drill-stings. Yoona took the spaceship through a shoal of small meteors and dusted them off. After that, they adapted the turret laser to a 360 degree turn and manned it non-stop.

Amebs were named after plate-sized, slithery things on Mars. These were giant-sized outer space versions, which could change colour and shape and grow as big as the spaceship. Reb was at the controls when the first one pounced and he saved Deepwater by broadsiding and accelerating before the thing took hold. It would have broken them in half.

Yoona was talking in a whisper. There was a humming sound from the quiet spaceship. She looked at Gret's control readouts, but let the girl sleep.

'We were all tired, all on twenty-four hour alert,' she said. 'But it got really bad when – when—'

Then Reb had prexed. He had been exploring the spaceship

43

and they lost track of him. Then Yoona found him in the below deck, across his bed and prexing. Prexes were like a dose of flu with a short, confused, dreamstate time before the kid recovered. But this one went on and on so Yoona brain-linked and found herself in my classroom at school – in the middle of a much fuller and longer prex than any of them had before.

Then she had held out a full thirty-six hours in the hope I would recover. She didn't want to give control to Bren (all his brains are in his fists), but she got very tired and the jel was due to burst out again.

'I boosted you out of it.' She spoke another course change and Deepwater lifted over a spiky, sharp, orange mass like broken glass. 'My fault, Re – Robbie.' She'd nearly said 'Reb'.

We were both silent. She had waited thirty-six hours after seeing me in the school, before boosting me? Earth-time and Deepwater-time were crazily different. Another puzzle.

'Why don't you turn back . . . to a galaxy somewhere . . . or another planet?'

'We've talked about it. Gret and Bren want to.' Her hand rested on the console. 'But Deepwater is on a course somewhere with properly-set directions. It's *going* somewhere and we have to see where that somewhere is.'

'You don't know?'

'No.' Yoona was looking at the knotted yellow strings of an exploded star. 'That throws the others a bit.'

'But not you?'

'Not me.' She touched another crystal. 'I have a feeling.'

'A feeling about what? About where you are now?'

'No.' Yoona spoke over the console and the spaceship turned aside like a well-trained dog. 'I have a feeling that Deepwater knows where it is going.'

All the information in COL's memory banks could not help. They were guiding Deepwater through an unknown, uncharted jungle of deep space. And I was on their spaceship, part of it, riding the colour-blackness to nowhere. I should have been even more scared, but I just found myself getting angry. One thing that Mum and Dad both said was never just wait for something to happen.

'So do something about it!'

'What?' Yoona shot me a puzzled glance.

'Do something about it, find out why you're here—'

'We have tried, but the door back to NUN is shut.' Yoona was getting angry now.

So what did all that mean? Ride Deepwater like a bike or a car – did these kids really know what outer space *was*?

'You don't realise where you are, do you?'

'Robbie, we've tried to find our star position—'

'Not that! Here – outer space!' I was shouting, but Gret kept on sleeping. 'Yoona, outer space is nothing, it's not somewhere to live! You're going nowhere – nowhere into nothing!'

'Robbie, we have tried—'

'Oh yeah, you tried to get through a shut door.'

I was remembering Dad when he lost his job. He took a week to talk about it, then he realised it didn't have to be the end, it could be a new job, new chances, somewhere better to go. Yoona opened her mouth to speak, but I got in first.

'So the door was shut. You were in that golden room, then you got into this one. Why – because somebody or something pushed you?'

'Pushed us to what?' Yoona's yellow eyes were wide and she looked very angry.

'Maybe to finding something *out*!' Like Dad had found out there was life after getting laid off. 'Yoona, if people push you around then push back.' Some well-known words came to mind. 'Kick some ass.'

'Kick some—?' Yoona thought I had gone mad.

I twisted round in my seat and pointed into the blackness. 'Yoona, kicking ass means finding out where you are. It means getting action going, it means – means getting off your *bum* and doing something!'

Yoona looked at me like I was a trite.

'Do something?'

'Yeah, you're not just here for the ride!'

There was another stream of the glittery meteors far ahead. A long way below was a wide, floating carpet of thin blue mist. Yoona was looking at me, really puzzled, thinking hard.

'Robbie . . .'

We were high above the blue mist, but even so it seemed to ripple with our movement overhead. It was rising upward.

'Hey, what's that?' I said. Yoona looked down and she moved very fast.

'COL, full engine thrust, vertical climb!'

She slammed a hand on the crystals and the siren screamed. Deepwater was already moving in a steep upward curve as, below, the 'mist' came alive, solid, slapping like a hungry blanket.

'COL, level course, starboard variant eight.'

Deepwater shuddered as though doing a tight corner. Bren was running down from the turret room. Zak from the below deck. The course change threw him against the side and he yelled with pain. Bren pulled him up and the hatch slid shut. A solid blue tentacle hit the window with a heavy, thwacking sound through the iron-glass. Another slammed over the top of the spaceship. Big though it was, Deepwater jarred like smashing into a wall, and nearly stopped.

The rest of the thing was rising with incredible speed in front of the spaceship. The laser cannon overhead fired, straight into the thick blue mass. It puckered and swirled but wrapped itself solidly over the window. I could almost see a formless, cruel face.

'COL, full engine thrust, reverse!'

Yoona was only just quick enough. Like a shark fighting the net, Deepwater backed and the laser fired again. The tentacles slipped away and we saw the whole blue 'thing'. I was looking at an ameb.

It rolled itself up, dark blue now, like a monster jellyfish. Lis fired the laser again and the yellow splash of fire hardly seemed to dent it.

Yoona was leaning forward, both hands on the console, her eyes strong and hard. Bren was rigid in his seat, Gret glaring with green-eyed tension. We were still moving backwards and another laser blast hit the thing. It folded, spreading blue jelly wings.

'It's had enough,' gasped Bren.

As he spoke, the ameb wrapped itself into a thick lump and rocketed straight at us. The next burst of laser fire just flicked off and it kept coming like a huge cannonball.

'COL, full ahead!'

Deepwater shuddered again and shot forward. Lis got in one more burst of laser fire and the ameb wavered. The blunt nose of Deepwater rammed it dead centre, going on through, tearing it apart. Two huge slabs of jelly slithered away on each side and Deepwater kept going.

'COL, maintain full speed,' snapped Yoona. 'Vision screen, rear section.' The screen flickered up and Gret gave a small cry of disgust.

Behind Deepwater, the two jelly-slabs were already sliding back together as the thing reformed itself. It was already moving back after us. There was another thud overhead as the laser cannon fired. Lis had trained the turret right round, but the ameb seemed scarcely dented. It came closer and the horrible tentacle-wings began to spread again.

'Boosters,' I said softly, the Reb-echo in my throat.

'COL, boost the main energy-drive, five seconds.' Yoona showed her teeth in a tight grin.

The ameb was nearly up to us again. COL charged the Deepwater engines with extra power and the blast of unburned energy shot out of the exhaust like an invisible torpedo. It slammed into the ameb, exploding it into a hundred pieces.

That was not the end of it, for you can't kill an ameb that easily. But by the time it pulled itself back together, we would be thousands of kilometres away. So it would have to choose another colour, spread itself out and wait for the next space traveller. We had escaped.

47

There was total silence on the main deck of Deepwater for a long time. Then Bren spoke.

'How did it get so close?'

'I was asleep,' said Gret. She rubbed green hands over her green face.

'And I was talking to Reb,' said Yoona. 'We stopped being on our guard for the wrong minute.' She was very angry with herself.

'So neither of our commanders can spot an ameb now,' said Bren, looking at me. 'Something's wrong.'

'Amebs are always difficult to screen, you know that.' Yoona was looking at me and there was a flicker of something in her eyes. She stood up.

'COL, Reb and I are below deck, advise all course corrections.' She gave me another of her tight, hidden arm-squeezes. Urgent, it said. 'All right, Bren, you can be in command for ten minutes.'

'In command without COL,' said Gret. She had recovered quickly enough.

'Then keep your eyes open. *And* the intercom,' snapped Yoona. She led the way below. The hatch closed over us.

Yoona stood for a moment, thinking. There was that flicker again in her eyes as she looked at me. She took two squeeze bottles off the rack and threw me one, then punched a button in the wall. A little metal slot opened and two thick blue biscuits tumbled out.

Mine tasted like sweet chalk. 'How are these things made?'

'I don't know,' said Yoona. She was still giving me those odd looks. 'COL or NUN must make them. They've just always been there.'

We sat down on our beds. Yoona bit a piece off her biscuit. She pulled her hair through her fingers. That was a bad sign – she was worried.

'Robbie, we call our spaceship Deepwater.'

I nodded. My mouth was full of biscuit.

'Lis makes jokes about it. Six kids alone in outer space, in trouble, in really deep water. But "Deepwater" was a name that all of us just *knew* from right inside our subconscious.' She paused, then spoke softly. 'A spaceship . . . in a deep, black ocean with no shores.'

They were in deep and very black water. I nodded. It was a good name.

'But I've never thought about why we were here. Maybe NUN did too much thinking for us.' She pulled a metal box from under her bed. 'Robbie, when I entered your prex—'

I didn't like being reminded of that. It sent a tingle through me. She was unclipping, opening the box. There was a lot of shiny hi-tech gear inside. She pulled out two headsets like for a Walkman. They had a tiny crystal disc in front.

'These are brain-scanners, in case we get a head injury. Lis prexed first so I put one on her and me, to check her head.' She fiddled with the headset. 'I could get into her prex, like share the experience with her, make sure she was all right. And the others. But when Reb prexed, I had to break it, get him back and—' She broke off again.

'And you got me,' I said.

'Yes. And you're making sense, you're right. We do have to know why. We have to start kicking some—' She broke off again with another funny look at me.

'Ass,' I said. 'What you sit on.'

I was trying to be funny but Yoona's next words scared all the jokes out of me.

'Robbie, you're going to prex again.'

8 Meatgrinder again

'What?' It was like she was wishing it on me!

'You are!' She was desperate. 'Lie down!' She began tugging my boots off. 'I can see it in your eyes.'

And she must have seen the look of horror on my face. She was right, I could feel that little buzzing that seemed to come from behind my eyes. I began to blink.

'Get out of it as soon as you can – I won't use the headset unless I have to.' She pulled the second boot off. 'Get out of it, try and make it work for you – there might be answers on Earth!'

'Yes,' I muttered. I think I spoke, but I couldn't hear my own voice. I felt sick. Yoona was still speaking, but everything was going like a blender again and I crashed back on my bed.

'Come back soon, I'll explain—'

Her voice cut. The blender spun in crazy, sick darkness and I rolled over. Yoona touched my cheek, and spoke. But it wasn't her voice and I knew that before I opened my eyes.

'Kiddo?'

I kept my eyes shut and Mum gave my shoulder another firm shake. I opened them. There was sunlight through the windows and the alarm clock was gone. I felt even worse.

'You're supposed to be at the supermarket, Mum,' I said. The buzzing was still in my head and the blender was going more slowly.

'Your dad phoned and said you didn't seem too well.' Yes, Dad had been giving me funny looks at breakfast. 'Come on, lunch.'

I followed Mum out. It was one o'clock. All those hours on

Deepwater didn't make sense against Earth-time. Mum had called here and got no answer. She she came home, found me asleep and took away the alarm. Then with her lunch-hour nearly over, she gave me a shake. And I had come back across space from Deepwater. But Yoona had known I was going to prex . . . from the expression in my eyes. How?

'Aren't you going to the pictures this afternoon with Dad and Sarah?'

I shook my head. Lunch was macaroni cheese, but I'd just eaten – on Deepwater – and I wasn't hungry. And my mind was still swirling with thoughts of Yoona, amebs, and all the wonderful patterns of Colour-space. Something inside me was kicking and bouncing. It was like trying to get out of prison.

'So can we talk about that problem, Robbie?' Mum glanced at her watch.

'What problem, Mum?'

'Mrs Burkitt's son,' she said. 'Connal.'

Mrs Burkitt's son? Connal? I could hardly remember which country I was in. Then I clicked. Meatgrinder!

'Yes, I know him, Mum.' After jel, trites and amebs, Meatgrinder was the least of my worries.

'Well, the parent-teacher committee' – she was on it, of course – 'has heard he's running some type of . . . scam.'

Yes, Mum, some type of a scam. Blood money, protection racket, extortion, the terms were simple. You played ten games a week at his mum's video parlour or Meatgrinder kicked some of your teeth loose and if that didn't work, he jumped on your head. Needless to say, he was the biggest kid in school and loved watching the horror films where everyone gets torn to pieces.

'Is he, Mum?'

You don't tell parents what happens at school. It's basically none of their business. And even if you did, Meatgrinder would get counselling, anger control, integration into the class structure – which means he would just wait a while before kicking the rest of your teeth loose and jumping on your head again. Parents do not understand about the real life of being a kid.

So I just shook my head. That means none of your business and Mum knew it. So, being clever, she changed the subject.

'The alarm clock. Sleeping in until one?'

'I only slept till one because you took the alarm away.' Did she think I lay awake all night worrying about Meatgrinder?

'All right. But if Connal is being heavy with the kids . . . well, we want to know for his sake, too.'

Parents are so blind. Meatgrinder wants to own a casino. You can't help kids like that.

'I'm going for a bike ride, Mum.'

'Connal's mum is a single parent. He feels very much about helping her, he's insecure—'

Meatgrinder was as insecure as an ameb. I was already heading for the door and Mum let me go. Parents can be understanding – and she was late back for work.

I got on my bike and pedalled down the drive. I didn't like being outside, but if I'd gone on talking to Mum I might have said too much. And Deepwater was my secret; it didn't belong to anyone here on Earth. I wanted to be up in the blackness and twinkling distant stars.

The bright sunlight burning my skin seemed wrong. The shopping centre was full of people and noise and that seemed wrong, too. I felt I was looking at it all through glass. Nothing was real.

What was it Yoona had said? I had to fight my way out. But how? A prex just happened and it might not happen again. That filled me with panic. I would be trapped on Earth!

Trapped? I took the bike round the back of the shopping centre, thinking hard. How could I be trapped like that – or was that the Reb part of me thinking? Then my bike stopped and was jerked round as someone stepped in front. Meatgrinder.

'Five games,' he hissed. There was an ugly scowl all over his fat face. He had on his black leather jacket, a signet ring with a skull on it and a T-shirt with crossed bloodstained axes.

Insecure – yes, like a mad gorilla is insecure.

'I'm not five games behind.' Even thinking from across the universe I had to survive. Reeboks was there, too. He had rich parents who wanted him to experience real life in an ordinary school – so Reeboks just got in behind Meatgrinder and lived a very safe life.

'We added two extra,' said Reeboks nastily. 'Penalty interest rates, Milkybar.' His dad runs a bank.

'I don't owe you a thing,' I said. I was thinking of Yoona ramming Deepwater into the ameb. 'Get stuffed.'

Meatgrinder snarled and I got off my bike. Reeboks squealed a 'gettim big guy' and I was one second away from a face full of knuckles. Then it was like another person exploding in me. Maybe it was Reb, maybe it was just too much hassle. But when Meatgrinder punched, I ducked my head, punched back and pushed hard. He went down and so did Reeboks behind him. I was full of a cold bad temper.

Meatgrinder was getting up. I let him – nearly – then pushed him hard and he went down on top of Reeboks again. It was very easy, too easy. Meatgrinder got up again and I grabbed his precious leather jacket. The anger boosted me like super-charged energy and I slammed him against the wall.

'I don't owe you anything.' My voice had a strong Reb-echo. 'Now don't give me any more hassles, Connal.'

I stepped back, ready to fight again. Reeboks was getting to his feet and I bashed into him. He went down again, yelling like he was being murdered.

Meatgrinder stood there. Calling him 'Connal' seemed to work more than anything, catching him off balance. And there must have been something in my face and voice. He wanted to fight, he was ready to. But he knew there was something wrong and he'd get really hurt. He snarled again.

'Nobody calls me Connal.'

'I do – Connal.'

I got back on my bike. Reeboks rolled frantically – into a puddle – but the wheels were at least fifteen centimetres away.

I biked off without looking back, even when a stone whizzed past my head. Reeboks, of course.

There were some kids watching. Meatgrinder did business in the carpark. Glyn Evans shouted out to me, but I kept going. And across the road, leaning on her handlebars, was Denie Miles. She gave me a very cool look but said nothing.

I biked on home. I was shivering now. That person-exploding feeling had all gone and my inside felt like an empty bag of crisps. Make it work for you, Yoona had said, there might be answers. All I'd done was hit a fat creep.

I left my bike in the driveway and went into the garage. There was a stack of cartons at the end where Mum put the recyclable stuff. I sat down. My head was aching again.

I was thinking about a girl with blonde and red hair. Even a boy with deep red dreadlocks, a green girl and a blue girl. Lis had done a really good job slowing down that ameb. The Deepwater kids were more real to me than anything else. All this was like a photograph.

Fight the prex. I could almost hear Yoona's sharp, impatient voice. I stood up and breathed in a deep smell of oil, petrol and rubbish. The garage was like a prison. I breathed in again very deeply, shut my eyes and tried to think myself somewhere else.

No good. I tried again, so hard that I nearly blew all my brain cells. Then I imagined I was in a runaway truck, speeding down the road. That didn't work either. There was no way out of this prex before it was ready to happen. If it even happened again.

I sat down. There were footsteps coming up the drive, but it couldn't be Mum yet, not unless time was speeding up again.

'Robbie?'

Denie Miles was standing there. Her bike was at the gate. The sunlight dazzled behind her, so brightly that I shut my eyes. She came across and the sound changed into a clatter of someone coming downstairs.

'Reb! Zak!'

I opened my eyes. Lis was there, blue face, untidy hair and

real. Memories of Earth disappeared like a flash.

'Yoona wants us all on deck.'

Zak was sitting up, rubbing his eyes. He must have come down while I was out of it. I began pulling on my boots. My track suit felt natural after the Earth-clothes. Zak looked over. There was a strange look on his face.

'Did you sleep all right, Reb? No more prexing?'

Had he guessed? Yoona didn't want me to say anything about the prexing, but Lis interrupted anyway. 'We might all want to prex. You just see what's up ahead.' She led the way up and I could feel Zak's eyes on me as I followed.

Everything was quiet on deck. I sat down beside Yoona and the hush went on for several minutes. We watched it and even before we knew what it was, we felt a sense of creeping horror. Deep space held a lot of danger, but we never expected anything as spooky and strange as this.

Ahead of us, very far off in the dark ocean, was a large spaceship. One end was shaped and the other ended in a huge round exhaust, set round the long, sharp fins. Lis was the first to speak and she only whispered.

'That's us.'

The ship was just like ours, floating like a ghostly twin sister in the blackness.

Another Deepwater.

9   Ghost sister

'Stations,' said Yoona.

Zak and Lis headed upstairs. Yoona waited until the turret was manned before she gave the next order. She spoke carefully and was very tense.

'COL, slow to minimum speed and bring up that thing full on the vision screen.' Thing. She couldn't bring herself to give it a name like Deepwater.

The spaceship came up on screen. It seemed dead and derelict, hanging before us without moving. There was a huge, jagged dent down one side where maybe a meteor had rammed it. The airlocks were open black holes, the observation windows dark eyes in a dead ship. Nothing could be living in that thing. Nothing?

'There could be a million trites inside,' whispered Bren.

'COL, circuit at fifty kilometres.' Yoona spoke into the intercom, 'Lis, did you copy that?'

'Copy,' said Lis. The turret cannon moved to centre on the derelict as we completed a full circle. There was no sign of life. We began another circuit.

'COL, full focus on the upper deck.'

Those dead, dark eyes sprang up close on our vision screen. I jumped a little. For a moment, not even that long, I thought I saw a pale, shapeless figure at the window, then it flitted out of sight. Yoona darted me a quick glance – she'd seen it, too.

'No life readouts,' said Bren.

By now we had nearly completed the second circuit. And we couldn't deny it, even if we wanted to. We knew what

Deepwater looked like, for we'd seen the grid pattern often enough. And that wreck was identical. It must have been built by whoever built our ship.

'So what do we do now?' asked Gret.

'Leave it,' said Bren.

'We must find out what happened.' Yoona was looking at the dark windows and I knew she was thinking about that pale, ghostly shape. 'If anyone is still alive.'

'No life readouts,' repeated Bren.

'The hull might be blocking,' I said with a little Reb-echo. Screening trites or even a whole ameb. Or another horrible alien creature that we knew nothing about.

'Yeah, and how do we get over there?' he asked. We couldn't take Deepwater any closer.'

'OMA,' I said.

Another little Reb-echo right from the back of my throat. And a very silly one, because I suddenly guessed who'd be in the OMA.

'Too dangerous,' said Gret softly, but she flicked Yoona a challenging look.

'Reb?' Yoona glanced at me.

OMA. Outside Maintenance Auxiliary. Deepwater had eight, four in each of the main exit ports and two big longboats somewhere down the bottom of the ship, but they were for emergencies. OMAs were two-seaters. I also knew – without thinking – that Reb and Lis had used one to repair a vent broken by the one mag-met that Lis actually missed.

Yoona was still looking at me, she was troubled and I found out why when silky-smooth Gret spoke again.

'Bren and I aren't cleared for the OMA. Lis and Zak are in the bubble, So . . .'

'So that leaves me.' I said. The dead, grey wreck hung in space before us. Even my mum admits I'm no hero.

'But you might prex,' Gret blinked her green eyes. 'Alone in outer space.'

'We'll go together,' said Yoona.

Bren looked at her, tensed, then pulled a dreadlock. He'd finally realised what clever Gret was leading up to. So did Yoona, she'd probably work it out ahead of Gret – also that she had no choice.

'I'll give Bren voice-access to COL.' She hated having to say that.

'I'll go alone.' And I hated having to say *that*.

'Nobody goes alone,' said Yoona. 'COL, copy Bren's voice to access control.'

She motioned him to the console and he stood up, swaggering a bit as he leaned over. 'Thank you, Yoona.' The console glowed red under his hand.

'Tell COL to line us up with that exit port.'

He did so, word-perfect, and gave another little teasing tug of his dreadlock. That guy really loved himself.

'And remember, inside or outside, I'm still in command of Deepwater.'

The grin went. There was a yell from upstairs and Lis came charging down the steps. 'Yoona, you can't leave that rockhead Jupie in charge. I'll go with Reb.'

'Shut up, you polar freakie!' shouted Bren angrily.

'Shut up, both of you!' Yoona's tension showed only a moment. 'Lis, get back to the bubble!'

She gave an upset look and went. Yoona beckoned me and we went below. The suit-lockers were inset between each bed. The space suits seemed just bigger versions of our overalls with helmets, life-packs and strap-on magnetic shoes. My Robbie fingers made a few mistakes, but Yoona quickly corrected them. Her face was level and set.

'Why?' I asked.

'There must be answers on that ship, and we need them.'

'Answers?'

'Answers to why we're here.' She gave a little tight smile. 'It was your idea, Robbie.'

Yeah, not actually a very bright idea. I was about to say – when Gret appeared in the hatchway.

'Tell Bren to begin airlock procedure,' said Yoona.

Gret nodded and gave us one of her funny blinking looks. 'Good luck,' she said. The hatch closed.

'Why is Gret wishing us good luck?'

Yoona clicked my helmet on. 'You don't understand Gret.' She showed me how to raise, lower and seal the visor. 'Neither did Reb.' She handed me a laser rifle.

The first airlock door hissed open and we clomped through. There were four of them before we reached the main port.

'Gret's used this to get voice-ac for Bren,' Yoona said. 'She's clever, she pulls his strings.' The second airlock hissed open.

'Why doesn't she like you?'

'Nothing personal, Robbie. South Mars quadrants were science and hi-tech, North Mars were miners and general works. Sandbrains, they always felt a bit inferior.' The third airlock hissed open. 'By the way, they don't like being called sand-brains.'

'Or polar freakies.'

'Lis is from Cydonia, near the ice-cap. Her skin tint was caused by the ozone or sun-filters or something, but everyone says they went blue with the cold.'

The last airlock was opening. My body tingled like electric shocks were passing through. We were getting closer and closer to deep space.

'Why won't you give them control?'

'Two in command is enough – was enough.' The airlock shut behind us. 'Don't worry, Robbie, they need us. Lis would sort them out if something happened.'

'She's a North Marshie sandbrain too.'

'North-*west*, Robbie. They're nicer.'

The exit port was bigger and wider. The OMA had already been pushed out of its metal cave and sat on its six metal legs, waiting. Two iron-glass cockpits stuck out like bulging eyes and a pair of long pincer arms extended like claws. It looked like a metal crayfish.

'COL, close fourth airlock,' came Bren's voice on the port

intercom and it shut. Now there was just one metal skin between us and deep outer space.

'Are you sure about this, Robbie?'

'I still don't know why you want me.' I sounded really weak saying that, but it was true.

'I want Reb,' she said. 'He knows more than any of them and he's in you somehow. Even mixed up in a bad prex, that's something.'

'Reb and I will try not to let you down,' I said like a hero. I closed my visor.

Yoona suddenly laughed. Her face changed and she looked like a happy kid for just a moment. Then she pushed me into the first OMA seat, her voice still laughing a bit.

'If you do and we get killed, I shall never forgive you both.' She was getting in her side. 'Press the green crystal.'

I did and the hatch sealed itself. Yoona sealed her side and waved at me through the iron-glass. 'Opening main intercom.' Her words whispered a warning in my helmet. Open line, so everyone could hear us. 'Bren, we're ready.'

We heard Bren instructing COL. The port opened into a neat black circle of outer space and at once Yoona operated the OMA. Its metal legs tucked up underneath and it moved forward like a cork floating away from a bottle. I turned to look back and Yoona's voice came at once.

'Keep alert for trites, Reb. And never mind looking back.'

We glided out. There was no engine noise and all the dark universe closed round us – no, it opened like a flooding black ocean that could drown us easily.

I don't know how time passes in deep space, but it seemed to take forever to cross the blackness. Nobody from Deepwater spoke on the intercom and Yoona was intent on the controls. I felt like a tiny sardine waiting to be eaten by a huge black whale. We were trespassers.

The other ship grew bigger. The silver-plate metal sides had hundreds of thousands of tiny drill-marks all over them. 'Trites?' I asked. I was still twisting my head round, looking for them.

'They must have tried to drill through the sides. We've got those marks on Deepwater, too.'

Yoona turned the OMA and we began gliding up the side to the open port like a crayfish to its hole. The dead spaceship towered like a metal iceberg, ready to roll over and crush us.

I looked over. Deepwater hung across the blackness, the observation windows watching us like huge yellow eyes. We couldn't see anyone behind them, or in the yellow bubble set over it.

I was very scared. There was too much to think about while Yoona moved us closer. This ship was another Deepwater. Maybe it had a NUN and six teenage kids who were taking it somewhere unknown. Would we find their bodies? And that pale form we thought we'd seen . . . was it in the dead ship, waiting for us? I was really scared and Yoona was too, I knew it. But we had each other and I felt a bit better knowing that.

Yoona turned the OMA round. We would back in, so as to be ready for a quick getaway.

'Deepwater, any sign of anything?'

'Nothing,' came Bren's voice and over that, Lis, a lot more anxious.

'I'm keeping a good lookout, Yoona. There's nothing on the scanners.'

'Thanks, Lis. Going in now.'

Yoona looked over and a gloved thumb went up. Then the dark sides of the metal cave closed round us like an open mouth. the OMA's metal legs unfolded and touched without sound on the deck.

We tried to look around, but everything was black. Yoona was clipping a torch to her wrist, to leave both hands free for her laser rifle. She clicked it on and the light flashed.

'Open, Reb.'

I pressed the green crystal and the iron-glass covers unsealed with a loud gasp that made me jump. We stood up and made to get out. I unslung my laser rifle and my magnetic

62

shoes clopped silently on the metal floor. I turned as Yoona did and she flashed her torch forwards into the blackness.

And I saw the things waiting for us.

10   Ship of ghosts

'Trites!' yelled Yoona.

The strap on her rifle broke as she pulled it off. Her torch arm flashed crazily off shiny wings, spiked legs and stalk eyes. They clung to the walls, floor and ceiling of the airlock passage, watching us.

Trites move quickly, too quickly for us to get back into the OMA. I was fumbling for the controls of my rifle. But the trites still waited, stalk eyes gleaming. I had my hand on the fire button and Yoona yelled again.

'No!'

I don't know how she stopped herself firing. I was filled with panic and fear and my hands trembled on the rifle. I must have guessed the same moment she did, or I would have fired. Bren's voice buzzed in the intercom.

'Get out of the port, get out!'

'Wait!' shouted Yoona. That meant me, too. She extended her torch-wrist again and flashed the light over the silent, horrible things. None of them moved, but the stalk eyes glinted in the beam.

Then she took a step forward. And that made her just about the bravest girl in the universe.

'Yoona, Reb, get out, I'll zap them!' Lis was crying with distress in her intercom.

'They don't need to be zapped,' Yoona said.

She put one metal-soled shoe on the nearest trite. It collapsed in a shower of dust. I managed two steps forward and could almost hear the crackly sound as another scrunched into pieces.

'Dead,' whispered Yoona.

'All of them? Are you sure?' I wasn't.

'They'd have got us by now.' There were trites as far as her torch could flash and even dead they looked horrible.

'Deepwater, we're entering the airlock passage.'

'Copy.' The tension in Bren's voice came across the intercom.

We began walking into the blackness. The dead trites collapsed under our boots. My hand brushed one on the wall and it fell off. I jumped, and Yoona put out a hand. Steady, it said. Then her torch lit up a set of buttons. She pressed one and light flickered on from somewhere. I jumped again.

'Systems are still working.' Even Yoona sounded surprised. 'Probably running on the reserve batteries.' Solar-charged spaceships take a long time to die.

She kept pressing buttons as she went through each open lock. The lights flickered again as though they were running on the end of power and the dead trites watched us from their shadows. One fell from the ceiling on to Yoona's helmet. Its stalk eyes snapped as she dashed it away. I heard a little gasp through the intercom, the only sign of fear she gave.

We were at the deck-entry airlock now. The trites had stopped scrunching underfoot. Yoona led the way through into the lower deck. She thumbed a light switch and the same half-light shadows began to dance. Then she really scared me because she used a manual control to shut the deck-entry airlock, closing us in.

'Hey!' I shouted.

'We don't want live trites following us into the spaceship.' Yeah, that made sense. Yoona looked around and spoke to Deepwater. 'Below deck. Nothing.'

There were eight bunks just like ours and everything was set out exactly the same. There was no sign of anyone, no life except for a single dead trite in the middle of the floor. I made sure that got trodden on.

'Nothing at all?' came Bren's voice.

Yoona kicked a bed, then stamped her metal-booted foot on

the floor. I heard the dull clang through my helmet. 'The spaceship is still generating air,' she said. You can't hear noise in a vacuum. 'Not enough, so keep your visor sealed, Reb.'

Some air and some light, but the whole place still felt silent and dead, full of invisible ghosts hiding in the shadows. Yoona was checking the lockers, which were empty. I held my rifle tightly and she gently pushed my hand a little way from the fire button. Relax, Robbie, it said. Then she pointed her torch hand to the steps leading to the upper deck. The hatch was closed.

Then she looked at me. The silent question was obvious. Did I want to go on?

I didn't. No way in the wide galaxy did Robbie Mikkelson want to go up those steps and face any horrors that might be waiting. So I did the only thing I could. I nodded.

'Nothing below deck,' said Yoona to Deepwater. 'We're going up.'

I couldn't see her face behind the mask, but I could hear her loud breathing on the intercom. I wasn't the only one scared, but Yoona would rather die than admit that. Her foot clanged on the metal button and the hatch slid open overhead.

There was only a neat square of darkness above. No sound, nothing. Yoona swung her rifle to the front and began walking up the steps. I followed . . . and I still had that terrible feeling that something evil was waiting for us at the top.

Yoona paused at the top and swung her rifle round. The flickering lights below outlined her. Her voice whispered across the intercom to me and Deepwater as I followed her up.

'Nothing.'

As she said it, I saw the thing. It was white and somehow shapeless, seeming to pounce on Yoona with horrible flapping arms and legs.

I thumbed my laser and the blast jolted my arm. A pencil-thin jet of yellow light stabbed up, catching the white thing and hurling it back. I ran up the last steps, breathing so hard my mask misted.

'What was that?' came Bren's shout.

Yoona had already pressed the lights and opened the upper deck to the same flickering shadows.

'Nothing,' she said. 'Reb was just being careful.'

There were two more of those white things floating in the air and even in the half-light they looked as horrible as the first one, which I had blasted over a control chair. They were empty space suits, floating in the near zero air, their boots holding them in place. The movement of the hatch opening flapped their empty sleeves. Yoona looked over. Her breathing was still loud.

'Space suits,' she said. 'They must have broken loose from the lockers.'

They hadn't. No space suit stands upright when it breaks loose, but there was no point telling the others yet. The feeling of evil grew.

Yoona nudged one of the space suits with her laser rifle. Then her breath caught and she took a quick backward step.

I clomped quickly over. For the first time I sensed real fear. She looked at me, then silently pointed to a name stencilled in black letters on the space suit front. I could read it clearly in the flickering light.

Another of the empty suits was flapping just behind. Both were adult size. Yoona walked around the first one – not letting it touch her – and prodded with her rifle barrel at the second suit. Another black-stencilled name.

Yoona cut her intercom button to Deepwater.

'Robbie,' she whispered. 'We can't tell the others about this yet. Not over the intercom.'

I nodded and she connected agan. Bren's voice came over at once, sharp with suspicion.

'Why did you cut communication? What have you found.'

'Nothing, Bren,' lied Yoona. 'Accident, still checking the deck.'

She had to lie. There was no way of telling Bren over the intercom that she was looking at a space suit with his name over the pocket in clear large letters: BREN.

The name on the first suit was ZAK. We untangled the one I had blasted. Another name we knew, in big black letters: GRET.

'Still checking, Bren,' said Yoona. Only to break the silence.

Checking. The upper deck of this 'Deepwater' was empty and the consoles cold as tombstones. Up the steps in the turret room another empty white statue swayed, arms out as though for a horrible embrace: LIS.

None of this made sense. And there was no sign of anything that might have destroyed the crew, not even trite drill-marks on the iron-glass. Through it I could clearly see the yellow lights of our Deepwater. I went below again.

'Whoever was in here must have gone before power faded,' I said. 'Otherwise the trites would have bored in.'

'They went outside the spaceship and left the airlocks open?' said Yoona. No, that didn't make sense either. The trites had got in through the airlock. But even trites died on this dead ship. What had killed them?

And those space suits – standing on the deck as though alive, boots strapped on, gloves zipped, helmets sealed. But empty, as though the people in them had deflated like air from a balloon. And where were the space suits with the black-lettered names of REB and YOONA? This was a ship of ghosts.

We went below and Yoona stamped on the deck button. The hatch slid over, leaving those ghostly white things to themselves.

'What's your next move?' said Bren.

He knew. So did I and all the silent listeners on the Deepwater intercom – Yoona before everybody else, I'm sure. But she wanted to check the upper deck before she even let herself think about flashing her torch through the flickering shadows to the door at the other end of the lower deck.

It was the door that had been shut those many months on Deepwater, for so long that they had learned to live with it. The door that led to NUN. Yoona shone her torch on it for what seemed a very long time, then whispered into the interom.

'The NUN door is open.'

There was a long, long silence before Lis spoke.

'Yoona, Reb, come out of there.'

More silence. I could hear Bren and Gret whisper, then Bren louder, into the intercom again.

'Yes, Yoona, you'd better come out, it's dangerous. Never mind the answers.'

Bren was repeating the words that clever Gret had whispered. They were like flicking Yoona in the face because Bren knew – everyone did – that we needed those answers and they were somewhere in the haunted darkness of this Deepwater. Yoona knew that, too.

'Very kind of you to say that, Bren.'

She clomped over and nudged the door open. She didn't look back – if I didn't want to follow, I didn't have to. And I didn't want to. Right now I was the universe's most freaked-out kid, feeling a million times worse than when I was writing a rude poem about the principal in the school toilet and found out he was standing behind me. Come on Reb, I need you, I whispered to myself and my shoes began to clang after Yoona's through the open door into the dark passage that led to NUN.

The air seemed thicker here. Our shoes made a clanging that started up echoes before us. More half-lights came on and the grabbing dark shadows stayed just ahead of Yoona's torch. Silence everywhere, around us, between us and from Deepwater – a black, dead silence and the long passage seemed to have no end.

On and on it went. We were moving into the unknown heart of the spaceship, further and further from the safety of our Deepwater. It closed round us like an endless metal tomb with darkness on either side. Whoever built these Deepwaters did a simple, straight job like a prefabricated house; everything was planned in a big hurry and there was no time for designer styles and anything up-market. Who were they and why did they put six kids on their super-spaceship? Or was it all a terrible accident? Maybe all this was just a terrible dream.

That really made me scared. My breath misted in my helmet because I thought about prexing and a prex was the last thing Yoona needed right now. It was strange, though, I realised I was more afraid of prexing than I was of this giant, lonely spaceship. Then Yoona's torch flashed on another closed door. There was a circle stamped on it with a small V-nick on top and the symbols inside.

'We're at the door,' said Yoona to Deepwater. Everybody heard her and nobody spoke. She pushed it with her foot. 'It's open.'

'Careful,' said Bren.

Yoona's torch flashed on my face for a moment. She didn't speak, but she lowered her rifle and held out her free hand. I took it and held tight. It was a silent way of saying 'we're together', even if I wasn't the one she really wanted there. She pointed to my rifle.

'Cover me,' she said.

Then she kicked the door open and darkness oozed out round us like a slowly clutching hand.

11　The place of NUN

The place where their lives began. That's what she had said about the golden room on Deepwater. And this place of darkness was the same room – even I felt that. Yoona stepped into the middle of the doorway, but her torch was like a lost glow-worm in the darkness ahead. She raised her rifle and, without looking back, stepped over the threshold.

The sudden half-light shadows pounced again. The room's lighting system had turned itself on. Yoona stopped and I forced myself to walk through the door and stand beside her.

The place was big, and the half-light shadows made it huge. You have to imagine one of those outdoor stadiums where they have major football games or music festivals. Then, imagine it roofed over like a church and full of dark shadows. And then imagine being alone inside it, the middle chamber of this dead, dark spaceship. So we began walking into the centre of all this flickering darkness, and every step of the way I wanted to turn and run out as fast as my magnetic shoes would let me.

Yoona stopped again and unsealed her visor. She lifted it, took a quick sniff and shut it. Then she opened it again and took a deeper breath.

'We can breathe the air,' she said.

'What can you see?' came Bren's impatient voice.

I lifted my own visor as Yoona flashed her torch round. The air was thin and very cold and sent little quivering chills through my body.

'Nothing,' said Yoona. She was still flashing her torch. 'It seems the same as Deepwater . . . but empty.'

There was silence on the intercom. They were all thinking of their happy golden life, full of dreams come true. Bren began to speak and another voice interrupted, breathless and desperate. Zak's.

'What about NUN? Is there a NUN there?'

'No, Zak. This place is dead, like the rest of the ship.'

'The magic cave?' Another faraway intercom voice, this time from Lis. Another dream-memory in the way she whispered.

'No, Lis.' Yoona had already shone her torch into the open, lifeless terminal.

'Nothing.' No dreams in Gret's voice, just a flat reality.

'No—' Yoona stopped and gasped.

I flinched too, a long freezing tingle of horror. Yoona's torchlight had reflected suddenly on the solid outlines of long boxes. They flashed and glinted crystal in the darkness.

'What – what is it?' Bren's voice was rough with tension.

'Wake-up caskets. Like ours,' whispered Yoona.

They had woken up in their golden room on couches like these, with lift-up crystal covers. But these covers were shut on this ghost-ship with empty space suits and no people. Six of them, not eight. They looked like a row of black coffins.

'We'll check them,' she said.

Cold, dark shadow-fingers snatched at us as we walked over. Our clopping metal shoes were caught in the echoes like an army of unseen horrible phantoms marching round us. Then Yoona turned, her hand out for me to stop. Then a gloved finger pressed to her lips, meaning 'keep quiet'.

I think that even then Yoona had guessed what this dead ship was all about. That something so terrible had happened here, she didn't dare tell the others – or take the chance of me saying something on the intercom. She only trusted her own emotions.

Looking at me, she backed up to each coffin. As she did, she held her torch-arm over and shone it directly down. The first four she only glanced at as there was nothing inside. Then she stopped at the last two. She shone the torch down on one, then the other. She froze and her breathing became a quick gasp.

Bren and the others heard it. 'What is it?'

Yoona put out a hand on the crystal lid to steady herself. She was swaying, though, as if about to collapse.

'Nothing,' she said.

She swayed again. I took a step forward and her hand shot out. It was like getting a telepathic order. Stay back! Yoona had seen something that scared even her.

Then she stepped away from the coffins and walked back up to me. As she did, there was a little clicking sound and my intercom cut. So did Yoona's – I knew from the way her head jerked. There was nothing, utter silence. Then the lights flared a little more and a voice sounded in my helmet. It sounded tired, surprised, a little pleased and spoke one word.

'Children . . . ?'

That voice went through me like a laser bolt. My head began to spin. It was a voice I'd heard before, but not heard. It was not male or female and it sounded old, but still had enough light to be golden.

Something was buzzing behind my eyes. The whole flickering chamber did a blender spin, faster and faster. And as it did, it seemed to blaze up brightly round Yoona; a shimmering, blazing light that streamed off her like golden water.

It punched me like a golden fist and I staggered, the force throwing me back against one of the couches. I felt the bang against my helmeted head and I slid down, shoes scraping over the metal floor. Then blackness crashed over me like a trap closing.

There was nothing in the blackness but a horrible sick feeling of falling. The trap was opening again and there were two monster yellow eyes glaring at me. I scrambled up and my feet came easily off the floor because it was concrete and the open trap was the garage door lifting. Behind it, the yellow eyes were the headlights of our car. My father was getting out.

'Robbie – what the hell are you doing in here?'

Prexing again, and always at the worst time. It was the evening and they were back from the pictures with takeaways. I could smell the food, which made me sick. Sarah ran into the house, yelling that Dad had promised her first scratch at the card in the cartons that offered a trip for two to Honolulu and she was taking her ballet master.

I followed with Dad. Mum was there – she hadn't thought to look for me in the garage. Would she have found me? She also looked very grim.

'What's the matter, son?' Dad asked.

I was scared and shaking. Mum took one look and hustled me off to bed. I heard her talking to Dad before she came back with some of the takeaway on a plate.

'I've been looking all over the neighbourhood for you.'

I didn't say anything. The Earth-food made me sick. Earth-food? Was that what I called it? What was *happening* to me? And why should I feel that life here was totally strange?

'Mrs Burkitt's been on the phone. Apparently you went for Connal. And Mrs Hill, she says you ran your bike over young Graeme.'

And did she say Reeboks chucked a stone that nearly took my head off? Did Mrs Burkitt say that Connal started the fight? I should have trusted my clever mum, though. 'I did some phoning round. Mrs Evans says they went for you.'

I sat there and said nothing. The words pressed behind my lips, but I couldn't speak. I didn't need any of this and none of it mattered. Mother, I said silently, and I *never* called Mum that, Yoona is in deep space on a derelict spaceship and something awful may be happening to her. And she won't get back to Deepwater without me. And even now those horrible trites might have come back to life and be stalking down the metal passage on their spider legs.

And I wanted to know what Yoona saw in those coffins.

'Robbie!'

That was what Yoona called me. Robbie. And I was Reb too, but nobody on Earth called me that. I looked at her and for a moment she seemed scared, like I was a total stranger. Dad had come in, too. In the other room, Sarah turned the TV on loud.

'We'd like some answers, son,' said Dad.

'So would I,' I said, and I wasn't thinking about anything on Earth.

'What on earth do you think you're doing?' said Mum.

Nothing on Earth, I thought to myself. I tried to speak and the words scrambled like an egg. I nearly called Mum 'Mother' again. So I shut my mouth tight in case Reb began speaking.

They saw my mouth shut that special way. They stood there a few minutes more, but there was all Sunday.

'OK, kiddo. Are you coming out to watch telly?'

I shook my head.

'No pressure,' said Dad. Meaning they'd take it in turns tomorrow morning. The door closed. There were times when having socially responsible parents was a real pain in the bum.

That old feeling was coming back, like being split in half again, I could hear Yoona's voice with that desperate edge, like she was in the room – Robbie, if you prex make it work for you. How long could she wait for me, on a dead spaceship – and what was happening to her?

So I had to make it work for me. And I knew my prexing cycle now – it was with me for at least two or three hours. Maybe I could find something out, something that would help her.

Even as I thought that, I knew how futile it was. There was no way I could help Yoona across the universe and hundreds of years in the future. Unless I somehow unmixed myself from Reb and more and more I had a deep-down feeling that this would never happen. Reb and I were together for keeps.

My room was brightly lit. All my gear was here, my Walkman, hockey stick, tapes and tape deck. And it was crowding in on me; it looked strange and unreal, like – like a photograph. That room of shadows in the dead ship was more real than this. Maybe Reb was waking up there now – maybe it was all over.

I turned off my light. The darkness was better. I opened my window and let the cool night air blow on my face. Late afternoon had become night, like time was speeding up. And hundreds of silly little thoughts were chasing round my head, popping and zapping like a video game gone mad. I had to get out!

The noise from the telly seemed louder. Even the sound of my own feet was like clopping across the metal floor of the dead spaceship. I put a leg over the window and slipped out. I didn't know where I was going, I just wanted to be on my own to think, wait for a prex, wait for all the crazy thoughts to stop popping in my head.

I went round to the back of the house. The blinds were drawn, and behind them my family was living a normal life like I had a day or two ago. My bike was by the garage.

I went up to it. There was a footstep behind me and I made to turn. Something cold and hard touched the back of my neck and a voice behind me spoke.

'Don't make any sudden movements, Reb.'

The something cold and hard was very much like the barrel of a laser rifle.

12 Earth-time

I stood very still. It was a girl's voice, so that meant Gret had got into my prex. She was the only one I knew who would stick a laser rifle in the back of my neck. Was this it? Were she and Bren wiping out the competition?

Then the cold 'laser barrel' moved to my shoulder and the same voice went on.

'Sorry, I was tapping you on the shoulder and you moved.'

I turned round. Denie Miles was there with a bicycle pump in her hands. Her eyes were big and round in the darkness. I took a lot of deep breaths and let all the pounding in my heart stop.

'Denie . . . ?'

'I was fixing my tyre while I waited. I knew you'd be out.'

'Why did you call me Reb?'

'You called yourself Reb.' Her eyes shone in the streetlight. 'When you were in the garage.'

She slotted the bicycle pump back in place. I was still a bit thrown and my hands shook as I took the handlebars of my bike. I could still feel that cold touch on my neck.

'Are we going somewhere?' said Denie.

We? I looked back at her and my shaking hands let go of the handlebars. The bike went over with one of those crashes you could hear round the world. I pulled it up and shouted to Denie.

'Come on!'

The back door opened and Mum and Dad came out. Denie was already on her bike and I was getting on to mine.

'Robbie!'

That was Mum. I waved, gave Denie a push and she shot off down the drive.

'Going somewhere, Mum, back soon.'

'Robbie!'

That was Dad and his tone said you're not going anywhere, son. But I was. I kicked the pedals and raced off down the drive. Denie was ahead of me, whizzing through a pool of streetlight, round the cul-de-sac and down the road. Dad and Mum were shouting after us, her name as well as mine – so that meant her parents would be on our case.

We stopped at the corner. Denie grinned and pointed. 'My place is about a minute away.'

'Denie, my mum and dad will be phoning your mum and dad in about a minute.'

'My mum and dad are out tonight.' She grinned again and led the way.

The phone was ringing when we got to her place. Denie pressed the answer-phone button and a bleep-noise moment later, Mum's angry and concerned tones and Dad's just plain angry tones were filling the cassette. 'Just send our son home if you see him.' Nothing said about them coming round. Denie shut all the blinds anyway and took me into her room.

Denie had a really fantastic room. It told you all about her, as soon as you saw it. There was a small telescope and a Moon globe and huge star charts and a self-defence chart that showed all the different ways to flatten someone – and made me remember how she had sorted out Meatgrinder. On the ceiling was a chart with silver stars on a black background. I looked up at it.

'Alpha Centauri, the nearest star,' said Denie.

'Deepwater is past all known star positions,' I said, then bit my tongue. The words had just slipped out, right from Yoona's journal disc.

Silence. I could feel Denie looking at me. 'Deepwater. You were muttering something about that when I came into the garage.' Then she said quickly, 'Would you like some coffee?'

I nodded. She started to make the coffee. 'What happened in the classroom, Robbie?'

In the classroom. Two days and an endless million black space-years ago. I shook my head like I didn't know because I still wasn't telling Denie anything.

'I was watching you,' she said. 'You looked up like you'd seen something. You looked a bit funny.'

She had lots of books, a big panda and a little computer. She had a set of planets hanging over the bed and they were moving a little. I think she spent a lot of time in her room. I watched the planets move and didn't speak.

'I was waiting for the class to end. Then – then there was a feeling that everything folded for a minute. You really did look – strange.'

Yes, well, Denie, I'd seen something strange all right, a space-girl with a laser rifle had come into my life. I watched the planets bob up and down. Why had Denie sensed this and not the other kids?

'So?' I couldn't think of anything else to say.

'Sugar or sweetener? Milk?'

I nodded for milk and she put the hot cup beside me. It was very quiet in the house and I had that sick feeling. I had to find out what Denie knew. And I had to get back to Yoona.

'Then, when you sorted out Meatgrinder in the carpark, it was like someone else was inside you, breaking out.'

'It was me, that's all.'

'No, Robbie.' Denie shook her head. 'You never stood up to Meatgrinder before. And I wanted to tell you how great it was. So I followed you home – to the garage.'

I felt a chill go through me like the cold black air on that dead spaceship. 'What did you see?'

Denie stopped and for the first time she looked a bit changed. Denie was one of those kids who never showed their feelings and always knew the right answers in class. Now she looked a little scared.

'Then I saw – like there were two of you. Then one of you stood up and . . .' Her hands shook a moment as she sipped her coffee. 'Everything seemed to flicker like a bad telly picture and you said . . . I'm Reb.'

A car passed outside and a reflection from the headlights gleamed on the ceiling, outlining the silver dots of Alpha Centauri. I shut my eyes. I had that horrible, sick, tired feeling.

'Then you muttered something about getting lost and Deepwater, then seemed OK again – like someone had pulled a plug . . . You asked me to go away and I did.'

And she'd come back that night because she had a funny feeling I'd come out of the house. Just a feeling, she said. And I got a feeling she was a little more scared than she wanted to show.

So like a dam breaking, I told her what had happened. I told her about my first prex and Deepwater. About the jel and Colour-space, trites and amebs, Yoona, Lis, Bren, all of them. NUN, COL, the dead spaceship and it all came out like a tape on fast-forward.

Denie didn't laugh or even look surprised. She just listened and listened, her big brown eyes fixed on me, her mouth a little open and her face pale in the darkness because she had turned the lights off. It made talking easier for me.

She only reacted once. When I mentioned how Deepwater had left behind the last 'island galaxy', she gave a little gasp and looked up at the silver dots of Alpha Centauri. Then I finished and she sat there thinking, still looking at me.

'Would you like some more coffee?'

'No thanks.' I still didn't know what she thought. 'I suppose you think this is just some crazy, weird dream.'

'I saw what happened in the garage, remember?' She was still thinking hard and she tossed her head a little the way Yoona did sometimes. 'And if this is not a dream, then that girl – Yoona – needs you back there.'

'I still don't know how it happens.'

Denie shrugged. 'Simple. You belong in one world at a time.

So all this is a dream-thing, or what happens on Deepwater is.' Oh sure, Denie, very simple.

Denie looked up at the silver dots again. 'Robbie, how fast does that spaceship go?'

I had to really stop and think about that one. 'Yoona said something about two, two-fifty thousand kilometres an hour. A lot slower sometimes because we have to turn quickly.'

'That's what's wrong,' she muttered. She had a little pocket calculator and was tapping in some figures. 'Robbie, your spaceship could not travel faster than the speed of light.'

'OK.' I wasn't sure what she meant.

'Light speed is three hundred thousand kilometres per second.' She stressed that – per second. 'Travelling *that* fast, it would still take nearly five years just to reach there.'

She pointed up at Alpha Centauri, the closest star. I began to realise what she was saying.

'Our galaxy is the Milky Way. Just to go from one end of the Milky Way to the other at the speed of light would take . . . a hundred thousand years.'

'Past all known star positions,' I whispered, another echo from Yoona's journal disc.

'To reach the nearest galaxies would take at least another hundred thousand years.' Her voice was soft but I knew what she was gently trying to tell me. That all this was impossible, that the Deepwater side was a dream.

'Past all known star positions . . .' She was still gentle. 'Your spaceship could not have a crew of teenagers on board.'

'Time-blinking,' I said. The words shot out like a pair of trites.

Denie's brown eyes went big and round. 'Time travel, time distortion.' She got up suddenly like her jeans were on fire. 'Yes, that would be possible. Theoretically . . .' She looked at me. 'The only way to travel across infinity . . .'

I remembered something else. The circle diagram of NUN. I drew it on a piece of paper and showed her. Somehow Denie was a lot more excited now, like everything was boiling inside. Then she stopped.

'Hey, what's happening, why am I believing this so easily?' She sounded angry with herself. 'Hey, Robbie, you look awful.'

I was shivering now and sick again. I had to get home before I was in worse trouble. And I had to get back to Yoona. Denie knelt beside me.

'I'd better get you home.'

'I'm billions of light years from where I want to be.'

It was a shock hearing myself say that. Deepwater was more real than home. But from the look in Denie's eyes, I think it was the first time she really began to believe me. She stood up.

'Listen, I'll call your parents. We can talk some more on the way home.'

'Thanks, Denie.'

She paused at the door. 'Yoona sounds incredible.' She went out and I heard her pick up the phone in the hall.

Yoona *was* incredible. But I might never see her agan. Maybe this time I was back for keeps. And it was all so horrible, so sick and bloody horrible that I groaned like I'd never done before. It echoed round my head.

'Come on, get up.'

Why was Denie pulling me off the chair? My feet seemed glued to the floor. Then I opened my eyes and Yoona was looking at me in the flickering shadows of the room.

'Robbie, we have to get back!'

My boots clanged as she made me take a step. Her face was very pale and her breathing fast, like she'd been running.

'We have to get out of here. The power's running down.'

She was pushing me towards the door. Around us, the flickering shadows seemed darker and darker, like a huge black ameb was blotting out the light and shadows. A heavy layer of night was forming overhead. Then, out of the darkness, something screamed and a monster skeleton hand came lunging down at us.

Yoona pushed me sideways. The 'hand' crashed on to the metal deck, shattering one of the crystal caskets. It was a fretwork of girders from the roof. There was more screaming

as tortured metal ripped apart and the blackness grew thicker.
Yoona pulled me up again and gave me another hard push.

'Robbie, run for it. I think the ship is breaking up!'

13 Ship-wreck

Another metal girder crashed down beside us. There were more of the screaming metal sounds like horrible, insane laughter. The metal deck seemed to ripple and jerk like a mad carpet and the blackness swirled down like fog as we ran. Rivets were raining down like hailstones.

'What is it – what's happening?' Bren's voice – the intercom must have somehow reconnected. 'The ship is shaking.'

'It's coming apart,' yelled Yoona. We ducked another swinging girder. We were at the door now, leading to that long, dark passage. 'Stand by.'

I'll never forget that run down the tunnel. The shadows were so dark now that Yoona switched on her torch. The magnetic shoes clanged us down with each step and the metal deck plates sprang underfoot with a loud cracking sound. The ship was shuddering, screaming with an awful drowning noise. Once a bolt pinged sharply off my helmet.

Then the ship seemd to wrench and twist. The same thought hit us both and we slammed our visors down as blackness came sweeping up the tunnel like an iron broom. The total vacuum of deep space snapped down like a trap closing.

We were below decks. We could feel the spaceship tilting as we clanged over – silent clangs now, as we could hear nothing. We were frantic with the thought of being trapped; the airlocks might be jammed, locking us in our tomb together with those horrible, empty space suits on the upper deck, flapping and shaking in their ghostly last dance. Those airlocks had to be open!

They were. Yoona's torch flashed on them, sliding brokenly back and forth. Now we were in the tunnel, the trite bodies crunching silently underfoot again. The last airlock slid open and shut before us. We reached it and there, black against the blacker circle outline of space, was the OMA. Now the deck was tilting more and the OMA floating over the floor and out into space.

I grabbed its crayfish tail just in time. Yoona wrapped her arms round two of the legs and we managed to open the iron-glass cockpits. We scrambled inside and the deck tilted again. Yoona thumbed the engine into life and the pincer-arms banged the sides of the airlock as it slid out. They must have seen us from Deepwater because the intercom cut into frantic life. It was Lis.

'Yoona, the ship – the bubble!'

On top of us, the massive side of the spaceship was turning over. The whole of this other Deepwater was rolling like a whale. The bubble room on the top had torn loose and, jetted by its own operating systems, bounced down the sides like a crashing iceberg. Yoona flicked the controls desperately over and the thing tumbled past, missing us by centimetres. One of the laser cannon scraped down the side of my iron-glass cockpit as our tiny OMA sped away from the dead, black bulk of the spaceship.

Even so, another claw of girders nearly snatched us. The spaceship was shaking as though some force inside was exploding outward, tearing it apart. A huge section of side-plating sailed past, then smaller pieces and Yoona twisted the OMA frantically to avoid them. One hit would be fatal. We were in bad trouble and our Deepwater was a wide river of black space away. Yoona was as calm as ever as she snapped an order into the intercom. The safety of Deepwater came first.

'Bren, keep clear.'

The bows of Deepwater were already swinging as Bren moved it back for a quick getaway. Another mass of side-plate unrolled itself and exposed skeleton ribs of steel. One of the

OMA pincer-arms was knocked clean off by a chunk of wreckage. We were clear of the side, but still too close. The next roll and power-burst explosion would scatter chunks of metal at us like a broadside from a shotgun. Yoona gasped and shouted.

'Bren, no!'

Deepwater was moving towards us into the danger zone. It was moving quickly, directly at the death-struggles of its dying twin. Bren's voice came flatly on the intercom.

'Lining you up with the airlock – quick!'

Even as he spoke, Deepwater was closer. Yoona stopped twisting the little OMA through the deadly shower of fragments and opened to full power. We shot directly across into the path of Deepwater. Another chunk of metal shook the OMA and my iron-glass cockpit starred, then splintered and broke.

Deepwater was looming up. The airlock was in line and Yoona had only one chance. She angled the OMA round and as she did, a chunk of metal hit the side of Deepwater. Yoona gasped as though it had hit her. The spaceship held course. We were nearly there when something hit us and jack-knifed the OMA round. We would miss the airlock – this was the end. Nearly the end, for the little Reb-echo was back in my throat as I shouted.

'Yoona, the RAC!'

RAC, Remote Automatic Claw, the one left, on her side. Yoona plunged her hand into the sensor glove and squeezed tight. Just as Deepwater swept past, the metal arm-claw shot out and gripped the side of the airlock. It was nearly jerked out of the socket. Then we were being pulled along, like a crab hitching a ride on the side of a whale.

Another hunk of metal smashed into us but Deepwater was moving very fast and it was the last. Iron-glass from my cockpit tinkled round my helmet and Yoona looked over.

'All right?'

I nodded. Bren's voice crackled in the intercom again.

'Just getting clear. Hang on.'

'Don't worry, Bren, we're not going anywhere.' I thought for a moment that Yoona was making a joke, but her voice was quiet and oddly lifeless.

Deepwater was turning in a wide circle and slowing down. I looked through the broken iron-glass to the other side of the black river. The other Deepwater had nearly destroyed itself. It rolled again and the last of the plating fell away like scales from a dead fish. Inside, the girder-sections were knotting themselves like string. The huge exhaust pipe tore loose and something else seemed to explode behind them, scattering a huge cloud of brilliant dots like rainbow confetti. It was the energy from the solar banks, the last beat of a dead heart.

I heard Yoona choke, then give a little moan of horror. I was choking, too. It was awful to watch the huge ship shaking itself into wreckage and all of it in utter silence, like a black and white film with the soundtrack gone. There is no noise in deep space, but I could almost hear those last silent screams dying away. The danger was past and Deepwater nearly stopped. I spoke into the intercom to Yoona.

'We'd better get into the airlock.'

There was no answer. I looked over. Yoona was sitting in her cockpit, gloved hands over her face-mask and rigid like she was in shock. Even her breathing had stopped.

'Yoona,' I said. She didn't move.

'Get inside,' came Bren's impatient tones. Nobody else spoke. They were still watching that terrible sight of destruction.

'Yoona!' I shouted.

Her hands came away from her face-mask and I could hear her breathing again. She looked over, not at me, but at the wreckage I made myself take one more look and wished I hadn't.

There was nothing left that looked like our own powerful spaceship. The girders were broken like matchsticks and only the control section held some shape. It lay in a puddle of its own silver-plate scales and nearby the bubble room floated upside-down, like a shattered egg. Above it, the cloud of energy dots, millions and millions of them, formed a rainbow arc over the wreckage.

'Yoona, it's over,' I said.

'Inside!' came Bren's sharp voice.

Yoona didn't seem to hear either of us. But I saw her hand come out and the pincer-claw unclipped from the side. The Oma turned, tucking itself neatly back into the safe darkness of our own Deepwater. The port hissed shut and the air pressure light glowed.

I waited a moment, then unsealed my visor. The first airlock door was already opening and Bren's voice came through clearly.

'On deck.' His voice had a strange shut note that made me uneasy.

Yoona hadn't moved. I went over and touched her shoulder. She looked at me through her face-mask like I was a stranger. I unsealed her helmet and lifted it off. Her face was white and there were tear-streaks down her cheeks from eyes red with crying.

'Yoona . . . ?'

She let me help her out. Her body was stiff, rigid and shaking. Our shoes clanged on the metal deck and the sound seemed to bring her out of it. She looked at me, then suddenly grabbed her thick hair and pulled hard. Her face set in one of those silent screams of hers, her mouth opened and blood trickled out from where she had bitten her lip. Then slowly, like an iron bar bending itself back into shape, she pulled herself together.

'Let's get on deck.' She reached out and cut the intercom. 'And nothing about what happened over there – I'll do the talking.'

There was something very, very wrong. What had happened on that ship was horrible and it was still catching up with me. OK, I was on my two legs, but my insides felt like an ice-cream in the microwave. But Yoona was different – there was a sound in her voice and a look in her eyes. Last year Mum lost two of her best friends in a mini-bus smash-up with a drunk driver, and she looked like that for a while.

Something had happened to Yoona on that ship while I was prexing. I remember that moan she gave when it exploded, as though she'd been really badly hurt and nothing made sense, nothing mattered.

'Did you hear me?' Her voice was sharp, her eyes glittered. Then she turned and clanged into the airlock passage.

We took off our space suits below deck. Yoona was still very uptight, her face flushed. She threw one of her metal overshoes against the wall with a force that reminded me of how Mum smashed a coffee cup the day of the funeral.

'Yoona, will you tell me what happened?'

Yoona squirted some water from a squeeze-bottle into her hand. She rubbed it over her face and blood-stained lip. She blinked like she was dazed and shook her head.

'No . . . I can't tell you anything yet. Not yet.'

She rubbed her hands over her face again, then stamped her foot on the deck button. The hatch slid open and she went on up without looking back. It was then I realised that none of the others had spoken to us for a long time.

And in about one minute, I knew why.

14   Rebellion

Nobody turned to us or spoke as we got on deck. Bren had Deepwater on automatic and he was standing with Gret, watching the wreckage of the other Deepwater in the distance. It was already far off, because our ship was moving with that gliding sensation of top speed.

'Thank you for saving us,' I said.

'You handled Deepwater very well, Bren,' said Yoona. Her voice had a flat sound to it. She looked pale and tired.

'Bren handled Deepwater as well as you,' said Gret.

They turned and came over. Bren said nothing, but gave a little tug of his dreadlock. There was a fixed, defiant smile on his face and he put his hand on the console.

'COL, holding pattern,' he said.

Yoona didn't try to grab the console. She took a step back and her voice was very quiet as though for a moment she didn't know what was going on.

'What happened over there?' Gret threw out the first challenge in that deadly quiet way of hers.

Yoona said nothing. She blinked several times and put a hand on the control chair.

'You were out of communication for three hours!'

'Three hours?' I never meant to speak, but like the worst dumb kid I let that slip out, that I hadn't known the time was passing. Gret pounced on it straight away.

'You were prexing again!' The green eyes flashed. 'You're still that Earthkid!'

There was a movement behind us. Zak and Lis had come

down the stairs. Zak paused for a nod from Bren, then went below deck. There was something sneaky in the way he moved and I should have followed. But I was more worried about Yoona. She spoke with the same flatness in her voice.

'Lis and Zak shouldn't be out of station.'

'I told them to come down when you were on deck,' said Bren. 'Deepwater's in a holding pattern.'

'We'll be all right, Yoona,' said Lis. 'No cover for trites here.'

That was true. Bren had taken us into a deep, empty gulf of space with open blackness all round.

'Bren only gave orders while I was off Deepwater,' said Yoona. Her voice was still flat, even slightly unsteady, as though she was thinking of something else.

'Yes, Yoona's back and she gives the orders,' I said.

'Not until we get some answers.' Bren looked over as Zak came up from below deck.

'All right, Bren, what are the questions?' There was a slight flush on Yoona's pale cheeks now.

'Why did you cut intercom? Zak checked and they're working.'

'I don't know.' She hesitated and put a hand up to her face a moment. 'It was an instinct, a feeling—'

'And then the same instinct said keep it off for three hours?' Gret that time.

'They were cut off for three hours,' said Zak, point-scoring for his mates. But it was Lis, without meaning to, who said the most damning thing.

'Before we lost contact, I thought – we all thought we heard something.'

'NUN!' said Zak eagerly.

The NUN voice. So much a part of their lives and the only thing that would ally them all to challenge Yoona. Especially when they had just seen a sister spaceship break up like a plastic model someone had stepped on.

'There was a NUN voice. But it only lasted a moment. It

94

had no power left . . .' She wasn't telling the truth, even I knew that. And I knew there was something wrong with her. So did Gret, judging by the way she was looking at Yoona.

'You could have restored the intercom,' she said softly. 'Got us to help. What else did you find?'

'Yoona?' said Lis. She was open-mouthed and could not believe Yoona would hide anything from her.

Yoona said nothing. I put my hand on her shoulder. Her body was rigid and trembling.

'Listen, we've just been through a hell of a time over there. Can't your questions wait till later?'

Bren was about to speak and Yoona interrupted. 'I'll tell you what happened when I'm ready. Until then, I'm still in command of Deepwater.'

She half closed her eyes and swayed a little.

'No,' said Bren.

'I can instruct COL to override you!' said Yoona with a flash of spirit. But there was something wrong. The old Yoona would have flattened Bren by now.

'And Bren can instruct COL to ignore. COL might blow a circuit,' said Gret. Oh yes, she and Bren had rehearsed this, but she was right.

'I'm in command,' repeated Yoona, but she was just about sleep-talking.

'Tell us, Yoona, please!' shouted Lis.

Yoona shook her head. 'Can't . . .'

'Then you don't get back control of Deepwater,' said Gret.

'We never agreed on that!' cried Lis.

'We made her captain, but now a majority don't want her!' Gret again, but I saw Zak nod.

Yoon shook her head, but slowly, like she had a terrible headache. Zak and Gret had moved to stand beside Bren. They just looked at her.

'We don't trust you,' said Bren, slapping her in the face with his words.

'I do.' Lis walked over to stand beside Yoona.

'So do I,' I said. 'Three against three isn't a majority.'

'Prexing Earthkids don't count,' sneered Bren.

'How would you like to prex to Ceres – the hard way?' I put up my fists and so did Bren. He stepped forward, snarling like Meatgrinder, but Yoona put up a hand.

'I'll tell you later.' But she was nearly talking to herself.

'Then you might get command of Deepwater back – later.' Bren put his hand on the console and it glowed red as if listening.

Yoona shut her eyes again and swayed as though about to fall over. I took her arm. 'I'm taking you below.' She just nodded. Lis took her other arm.

'Bubble room, Lis. We scanned a shoal of mag-mets, remember,' said Bren.

'I'm helping Yoona first—'

'Do as you're told, you stupid sandbrain,' whispered Yoona.

Lis stepped back, really hurt. It was like all the steam went out of her as she turned and headed up the steps. Nobody else spoke, but the moment we were below deckline Zak ran over and stamped on the button. The hatch slid shut over us. I helped Yoona on to her bed. She was flushed and breathing in quick, shallow gasps.

'Why did you say that to Lis? She was only trying to help.'

Yoona looked at me, her eyes unfocused. She moved her lips several times and I heard one word . . . 'explain' . . . then she lay back and closed her eyes.

I splashed some water from a squeeze-bottle over her forehead. It was hot and I could almost feel her head pounding. Now she was unconscious and beginning to toss a little. Delayed shock from that horrible time on the spaceship – something worse?

I stamped my foot on the hatch button at the bottom of the stairs and nothing happened. I did it again, then once more and shouted into the intercom.

'Hey, that hatch won't open.'

'Shut up, we've got mag-mets to deal with,' came Bren's voice.

I was about to say something then I saw the deck button had been forced up and some wires pulled out. It was fused. Zak hadn't just checked the intercom. No wonder Bren didn't mind us going below – he was locking us in! I hit the intercom button beside the steps.

'Bren, open up!'

'Prex back home, Earthkid,' came Bren's mocking voice. Gret was laughing too, and I got really mad. It was lucky for them we'd lost our laser rifles on the other ship.

'Yoona's sick with something!' At least they didn't laugh at that. 'Maybe it's a virus and we might all get it!'

That moved them. I heard some whispering, then the intercom went dead and the hatch opened. Gret appeared, with Bren behind her holding a laser rifle.

'Deepwater's in flight again, so no problems – understand?' Bren wasn't pointing the rifle at us, but his tone of voice meant business.

I nodded. Gret came halfway down the steps and looked at Yoona. Then she came all the way down, brushing past me.

'Gret,' called Bren, 'If she has got a virus, we don't want to catch it.'

Gret ignored him. She leaned over Yoona. There was a funny look on her face, like concern and doubt. She touched Yoona gently on the forehead, then turned and headed for the steps again.

'What is it?' I shouted.

Gret stopped halfway up the steps. She gave Yoona that half-concerned look again, then her mouth tightened and she shrugged.

'She's all right.'

'She's not, she's sick.'

Gret looked at me, but all the concern went and she spoke in her normal sour-apples way.

'Earthkid . . . she's prexing.'

The hatch closed.

I must have sat there for more than an hour. The intercom

was now dead, shut off from the upper deck end. It suited Gret and Bren to have Yoona out of the way, and prexing was something that happened sometimes to them all. Overhead came the boom of the laser as Lis exploded mag-mets.

Prexing is supposed to hit you suddenly; you can't fight it very long, even if you realise what's happening. Yoona had known what was happening and she had fought it as long as she could. There was another secret bottled up inside her, something she tried to tell me just before she fainted into the prex.

What had happened on that other Deepwater? What was so bad she couldn't tell the others, even if it meant losing command – or being rude to Lis just to get rid of her?

Another hour went by. The laser cannon was booming every minute or so as Lis pounded her way through a whole shoal of mag-mets. I was really worried now because Yoona was getting worse. Her flushed colour was fading out to a chalky white and her breathing was so shallow that I could scarcely hear it.

I tried to remember Mum's lessons on first aid. Yoona had either no pulse or I was holding her wrist in the wrong place. I put my head on her breast and the heartbeat was as faint as her breath, and getting fainter.

I hit the hatch again and shouted and screamed for someone. But even if they heard me, Gret or Bren wouldn't leave control with magnetic meteors hurtling themselves at the ship like missiles homing on to a target. The laser kept booming and Yoona had almost stopped breathing. Something had gone very wrong with her prex and she was dying.

And I was helpless. There was nothing I could do. Nothing? There was one thing, and it came to me like a little Reb-echo at the back of my throat. I was scared to think about it, even to help Yoona, but it was something I had to do.

I unclipped Yoona's medical locker from the end of her bed. The little headbands were inside. I slipped one on and fitted the other over Yoona's red and blonde hair, on to her forehead. The Reb-tingle was in my body and my hands knew just what to do. I clipped the portable console on to my wrist and had to press my finger on the crystal to activate it. I fitted on Yoona's, but my finger stayed over the crystal.

I was really scared. But Yoona had waited in that dead breaking-up spaceship to help me when she could have saved herself. And even if she hadn't, I knew I had to do it – because she had done it for me. I had to go into Yoona's prex. I activated her mini-console and waited for something to happen.

This *had* to work!

15   *Into Yoona's prex*

Yoona's head was tilted so that her sleeping face looked at me.
Then her body shuddered and a glowing, intense speck of light
grew out of the metal disc on her headband.

It stabbed straight up and hit my disc like a bullet. A solid
chain of light linked us with a force that felt as if it had knocked
my brains loose. My head did the blender spin and now it felt
like all of me was being squeezed into the light, like a bright
sucking whirlpool.

Then everything blacked. I couldn't see or feel anything.
Slowly the darkness became light. I was floating for a moment
before my feet were on ground that squelched when I took a
step forward. The darkness became tall green shadows that
suddenly clicked into focus like a camera lens. I took another
step forward and the ground squelched again.

My feet were on a muddy path and on either side were tall,
green-blue plants that closed overhead in spiky red and purple
bulbs. They grew out of green-blue swamp-water on both sides
of the path. It was raining and fat, heavy drops splashed all
round.

Ahead, a path ended in steps going up and round until
they were hidden by the tall plants. I began to climb them
slowly, still trying to work out where I was and what I could
control. My feet seemed to touch the ground, but there was
a funny, invisible prickling all over me, like I was covered
in see-through cellophane wrap. Even the water seemed to
splash off me. Yoona had said a kind of forcefield protected
her in the prex. I couldn't smell anything, and I seemed to

breathe through the invisible cellophane.

I went higher up the steps. The swamp below looked bottomless. Something splashed among the plant stalks and I saw a scaly, thick, green body. A muddy pointed head looked up and slit, bulging eyes blinked in a flat face. A webbed claw-hand splashed muddy bubbles when it ducked from sight. I could see overhead now, and there was no sky. Only low, blue, thick clouds pouring down unending rain. I got to the top and something crashed in front of me.

It was like a thick steel girder from a construction site. In front of me was a wide, level area and, on it, the most fantastic construction I'd ever seen – a pyramid, about twenty storeys high and ending in a sharp point. It was only half-finished and covered with scaffolding. The sides that were complete were covered with a smooth silver-glass plate that looked familiar. They reflected the blue-green cloud cover. The other open side showed layer on layer of rooms like a honeycombed beehive. The green plants stretched like a spiky mat in all directions and over them ran a kind of motorway on stilts. It ended in the far distance at another half-built pyramid. From where I was, only one side of that flashed blue-green.

I began to walk across. The rain was falling heavily, but there were hundreds of people out working round the scaffolding on the unfinished part of the pyramid. They couldn't see me, of course, but I almost sensed it didn't matter – that they were too busy to notice anything.

There were men, women and children. Most were dressed in blue overalls that streamed with water, and all had breathing-masks over their mouths as though to stop passing infection. Most had blue faces like Lis. Some were yellow-brown, red-brown and green, and a few were black. Most had shaved heads, but some had hair in topknots or pigtails.

I was picking my way over cables and ducking round piles of girders. It was strange how they worked – not just hard, but in a hurry. They were cutting girders, stacking them, building more scaffolding. And even though I couldn't hear them, I don't think anyone spoke. They just worked. And some of them looked very sick.

Another massive, long girder crashed down and a dozen men and women jumped on it and began cutting it with laser torches. And that was strange, too, because you don't build something by . . . by . . .

Then I realised they weren't building the pyramid. They were taking it apart.

A big-wheeled truck rumbled past, towing a load of girders. Another branch of the motorway stalked on its high legs over the swamp and it was covered with two streams of moving vehicles. It ended at a square platform and a mass of scaffolding round a huge metal skeleton as tall as the pyramid. Even half-finished, I knew what they were really building.

Deepwater.

The girders were its bones. The steel framework of the deck was already in place, and those silver-glass plates were the skin. I remembered that other Deepwater, rolling in space, shedding its silver scales . . . I was scared, sick and lost, and I had to find Yoona!

She was here somewhere. I sensed it, and even seemed to always move in the right direction, like she'd left invisible footprints. I walked around piles of girders and huge lengths of piping. And people, people everywhere, their faces set and desperate like long-distance runners trying to finish a really hard race.

I walked into the open part of the pyramid through a door frame that was still standing. Four children staggered out, each carrying a section of the silver-glass plate. There were stairs ahead and this was the way Yoona had come. I could sense it still, and there was a terrible urgency kicking inside me – she was in here somewhere and I had to find her!

I stopped on the first floor and began to follow a wide passage round the side. The metal headband was hurting on my forehead and it was so strange to have people look right through me and walk on.

103

There were more signs of the sickness here. Ahead of me a woman with black skin and red hair collapsed on the floor; I couldn't help, so I had to walk round her. Two other women came running up and I skipped to avoid them. I was scared they'd run right through me.

I was at a part now where the silver-glass hadn't been removed. The passage and open rooms were filled with a blue-green light filtered from outside. Inside, the people lay on beds; they looked tired and sick. The air was thick and seemed glassy and I realised I'd not seen a smiling face.

I felt close to Yoona now and the feeling drew me on. There was another door ahead which opened as I came to it. The blue-green light streamed into the room as a woman came out. She wore a long green coat; her face was light yellow, and she had thick golden curls of yellow hair. She had a headband like mine and I somehow sensed she was a doctor. She paused at the door and looked back, her face set in a sort of final sympathy. Then she went and I looked inside. Yoona was lying on the bed.

There were two people with her. Both were adults and looked like her. The man was very tall with blond hair and a deep brown face. The woman had red hair and light red skin. Both had that same final look on their faces.

Yoona was wearing a long, sleeveless, green robe and she looked just like I'd seen her on Deepwater. Her eyes were shut and she didn't seem to be breathing. As I watched, the man gently unclipped a drip-feed bottle from her arm. He did it in the same final way and I felt a dreadful stab of horror.

Yoona looked dead.

Both the adults were crying now. They *had* to be parents. As I stood there, trapped and frantic, not knowing what to do, the woman opened a gleaming silver case and took out a little flashing tube. She pressed it to her daughter's arm and drew it away. A little speck of blood was left. Then she leaned over and whispered something in Yoona's ear.

I made myself lurch forward. I had to do something. I had

to *try*! I grabbed her by the shoulders and shouted, 'Yoona, your prex is going on too long' – nearly the same words she once said to me. 'Yoona, we need you on Deepwater.' There was nothing in her face and I shouted again, 'Yoona, Bren can't fly Deepwater too long. We need you!'

I was yelling at the top of my voice and it was unreal. There was that little buzzing behind my eyes. Yoona was limp in my arms and the room was spinning. Behind me, Yoona's parents were putting the little tube back into the box. The air was so thick I could hardly speak.

'Yoona, Deepwater is in danger – danger!'

Just for a moment her eyelids flickered . The room began to spin and I put my arms tight round her body, trying to stop the prex from dragging me back. But it did – the same wrenching, the bright whirlpool spinning the other way. I had to let go of Yoona and I fell on to the hard metal floor of Deepwater.

My head ached and my body felt battered. Overhead came the boom-boom of the laser cannon as Lis blasted mag-mets. I had failed. I had to tell them Yoona was dead.

As I got up, she opened her eyes.

They were like a doll's eyes of empty yellow glass. She blinked and spoke without looking at me.

'Yoona is my name,' she whispered, like reciting a lesson to herself. 'My home is Py-Two, Orduna Set, south-east quadrant of Mars. My parents are Barla and Tem.' Now she was talking very fast, babbling. 'I have the spike-flower virus but I'm getting better—'

'Yoona, you're on Deepwater!' This was all we needed! The wrong Reb and now the wrong Yoona? 'Deepwater, on Deepwater!'

She stopped, her face pale. Overhead the laser cannon boomed. Suddenly she sat up, swinging her legs over the side of the bed. Life came back into those empty yellow eyes like sunlight. Then they blazed with hurt as though I'd broken a wonderful dream and she slapped me hard in the face.

Yoona was very strong. The blow knocked me back over

the next bed and it hurt like hell. She sat there, head down, hands clenched in her blonde and red hair like she wanted to pull it out by the roots. Then she looked at me.

'Robbie?'

Our Yoona – she was back? I tried to grin, but it hurt. So I gave her a squeeze-bottle but tried to stay out of strike-range while I handed it to her. She drank some and squirted it over her face.

'I was prexing.' She rubbed more water over her face. 'We built Deepwater on Mars. I was there, but became sick from going too near spike-flowers in the pollen season and I was . . .' She paused, trying to think, '. . . I was very ill. My parents were crying, but mother whispered to me that I'd live again.' Yoona shut her eyes a moment. 'Then I fell into this lovely dark sleep . . .'

Then she woke up back on Deepwater and hit me. In case she took another swing when she found out I was in her prex, I tried to kick the headbands under the bed. But she stood up and saw them.

'You came into my prex.' Her face cleared as she remembered. 'Robbie, I hit you. I'm sorry.'

'It didn't hurt.' No, it was like having a soccer ball slamming into my face.

I told her what had happened. About the scaly thing I saw in the swamp. A klopper, said Yoona, an underground Martian creature, very primitive, that came up when the swamps were terraformed. 'You were right to come after me.' She was still pale but managed to smile. 'It was very brave.' She didn't ask about her parents. 'Thanks, Robbie.'

I grinned and went redder than Bren. Right then I would have crawled a kilometre over broken glass for Yoona. Ten kilometres.

Boom-boom-boom went the laser cannon. Lis was having the time of her life. Yoona looked up quickly and went over to the intercom.

'The intercom's cut at the upper deck,' I said. 'They're just mag-mets. We forward-scanned them, remember?'

'I know!' she snapped, worried. 'But Bren can't run Deepwater on his own!'

'He'll go on running it until the others trust you again.'

Then I started to get angry. Yoona was a really sensible kid and right now she was being stupid.

'Yoona, they all know something happened on that other ship. You have to tell them!'

'Robbie, I don't know all the answers yet.'

'That doesn't matter!' I was shouting now. 'Yoona, you run Deepwater because the others trust you, not because COL likes the sound of your voice. OK, Gret and Bren are stirrers, but they trusted you. So did Zak and Lis. Now they don't.'

Yoona was silent. Overhead the cannon boom-boomed and down here it was very hot. There was a strange smell of something in the air. She looked at me and it was like she had the whole weight of the spaceship on her shoulders.

'How can I tell them what I don't understand?'

'Yoona, what makes Deepwater work is all of us.' I squeezed her hand tight, trying to make her understand. 'We *have* to care for each other – that's why you came into my prex, isn't it?'

'And why you came into mine?' She smiled again.

'Yes. And the others would have done it, too.'

The laser cannon pounded like a drum and the room was too close and warm. That faint smell of something was stronger. Yoona's own hands went tight on mine and this time she grinned.

'All right, everything. Everything that happened on that other ship. They won't like it, I didn't—'

She broke off and her eyes widened. If it hadn't been for everything happening, she would have noticed that smell earlier. Because it was the only warning that the alien monster living inside Deepwater was filling the ventilation shafts again, ready to burst out.

Jel.

Yoona always moved quickly. Even as the smell grew suddenly stronger, she was across and stamping her foot on the deck button. The hatch didn't move.

'Zak disconnected it,' I yelled.

'No,' she whispered, and her eyes went to the ventilation grill.

So did mine. It was all like some nightmare replay of my first minutes on Deepwater. Zak had rewelded the iron bars and they were bulging out the same way, with the pressure of something behind. Then they all snapped and a stream of thick, red jelly spouted into the room.

And this time we couldn't get out.

16 The creature strikes

The jel spread thickly over the floor and began moving towards us with a horrible snuffling sound like a cat finding mice. It was at the stairs already and even if Bren opened the hatch now, we were cut off.

We backed to the other end of the room. The jel moved slowly, as though it knew we were trapped. It was building itself huge from the endless spout pouring through the broken grill. It swelled larger and larger, like a monster slobbery blood-red mouth.

The airlock door was behind us. Only COL could open the door and neither of us had voice-ac. My elbow touched something, a small glass panel set in the metal. Yoona shot a glance at it.

'Manual Emergency Control – move!'

Her elbow smashed the glass and the airlock hissed open.

We did a sort of incredible backward somersault and Yoona was on her feet again as the jel pounced. It seemed to know we were escaping. Her fist smashed the glass over the 'close' button and the heavy bulk surged up, slamming against the closing door. A thin edge of red jelly stuff appeared and began to force the door back open.

Yoona had already smashed the next manual control. There was blood on her fingers now. The door opened and we tumbled through. It hissed shut just as the full monster crashed up against it like a jelly battering-ram.

Red jelly it might have been, but the strength of that thing was incredible! The second door strained and began to open. I smashed the third button and we went through. The door shut and thumped a moment later – the jel was right behind us. The door began to strain and a thin edge of jelly appeared. It grew thicker. We couldn't believe it!

I smashed the fourth button and we went through. There was blood on my fingers now. This time we didn't wait for the jel.

'Come on,' shouted Yoona.

She grabbed my wrist and aimed a high kick at the emergency airlock control. The glass shattered and we ran through. Behind us, a band of red was already at the door but this last door was very thick and strong and slid shut with a heavy crunch.

We were in the main airlock chamber, one door from outer space and no escape. The little OMA still rested lopsided on two legs, both cockpits smashed open. The other OMAs were sealed tight in their hangars and we couldn't get them out without COL. Something thick and strong thumped against the door, but it held. It was heavy and solid.

'That should hold all right,' I gasped, nursing my hand.

'Does it matter?' asked Yoona with a grim smile.

She was right, it didn't matter. COL would automatically alert Bren to all the airlocks being opened. Bren would do a scan and see jel all through the lower deck and airlocks. And even if he thought we were still alive, there was only one way to get rid of jel – blow it out the main ports into deep space.

And blow us out as well.

Bren wouldn't wait, because that stuff would swell up and burst through into the main deck. So any minute – any *moment* – the port would open and that would be the end. It was a slightly better way to die than being eaten by jel, I thought. The airlock door thumped again. Yoona's hand went to the emergency release control and she tried to speak calmly.

'No sense in waiting for it, Robbie, I'm sorry—'

She stopped, because I put out my hand – that little Reb-tingle again, always when I was really stressed out. My body stiffened and I pointed at the ceiling.

'Those, the little holes round the lights—'

Light came from the six interlocking circles. But there was an oval of tiny holes round these that I hadn't seen before.

'Decontamination, to clean the air when we come in from outer space. Robbie, why—'

She broke off. Holes meant something behind them, maybe an airshaft – a big airshaft. If only we could reach it.

We both thought of the same thing at the same time, but I was closer. I ran to the OMA and stuck my hand inside the cockpit sensor glove that operated its one remaining claw. The pincer shot up and clacked together – centimetres short.

'Extend!' yelled Yoona.

She leaned over me and pressed a crystal. The arm telescoped and smashed into the thick circle-glass. It scarcely cracked. The door thumped heavily again. Any time now, Bren would open the airlock!

I worked the sensor glove like a boxer on telly doing short arm jabs – that's what my dad called them. I punched hard and fast at the same place. A crack appeared and some glass tinkled to the floor. Yoona was at the other side, working the control to limp the broken-legged OMA closer. Now I could shorten the arm and jab up with more power, right in the middle.

Something shattered and the pincer-claw closed round a metal frame. I made my own hand into a fist and pulled the pincer arm down. It was strong enough to peel off steel-plating and it pulled that grill out like a weed by the roots. There was open darkness behind.

The airlock door was straining hard and trickles of jel appeared like horrible red fingers.

'Go on, Robbie!' shouted Yoona.

'You first!'

'Don't be stupid!'

'I'm not, you're taller!'

'Oh—'

She leaped up on the OMA, then jumped in the air and

111

grabbed the sides of the torn-out section. She swung kicking for a moment, then pulled herself up, all the way in. Her track suit ripped as she did. She scrambled round for a moment and her voice echoed.

'We can make it!'

She leaned down, hair falling round her face, and reached for me. Then the door jerked open, and as it did I heard the whole room vibrate. The OMA slipped and crashed down – and so did I. The exit port was beginning to open!

'Robbie!'

I scrambled back on the OMA as the last airlock burst and the jel flooded through. Nothing could make me move faster than the sight of that horrible, slobbering, red tongue. I leaped up like my feet had rockets on them and Yoona clutched my wrists and pulled me up. Below, a red light was flashing and I glimpsed a thin curved edge of black space appear.

Yoona yanked me up into the shaft. My track suit tore and something gashed my leg. Below there was a ripple and a thick spout of jel surged up at us like toothpaste out of a tube. Yoona shouted.

'Hold tight!'

We clung to the edges of the grill as a sudden black howling wind slammed down the tunnel into us. The open port was sucking out all the air and it streamed down our narrow tunnel, hitting us in the face like an iron river. The jel had just reached the top of the hole and a red speck touched my hand, stinging like fire. Then it was sucked down out of sight.

The jel was streaming out into space below us like a horrible torrent of red slime. We could breathe, but only just, by opening our mouths to the air-blast roaring round us like an express train. Above us on the upper deck of Deepwater they would think we were dead. We nearly were.

Yoona was trying to scream something in my ear. We couldn't stay here and wait for the air to go. There were ribbed projections, like join-marks, every metre of the shaft, and we began to fight our way forwards into the airstream. Even keeping our mouth open, we could scarcely breathe. The air hit the back of our throats in jabs and we froze. I thought my jaw was going to fall off.

Yoona screamed at me again and nodded her head up. There was a circular port above and she raised a hand to push it. She nearly slipped back and I grabbed her, but the port gave a little. Struggling hard against the air current, Yoona forced herself up into it.

Yoona was pulling me after her. The shaft was as big as the last one, with just room for the two of us. Yoona started climbing the ribbed projections like the rungs of a ladder and I followed. Below us, the plate clanged shut and I hoped it was airtight. Yoona stopped a moment and looked down. Her hair was a tangled mass. She was white-faced and breathless, but she managed to smile.

'I like the way you punched out that grill, Robbie,' she gasped. 'I'd hate to get into a fight with you.'

'Likewise,' I said. My cheek still hurt from last time.

We were OK. Our track suits were torn, we had cuts and bruises and ached all over. But we were alive and there was air and even some light in the shaft. But the circular trap that let us in was a one-way thing to keep the shaft sealed. It had shut behind us and there was nothing to open it this end.

'We can't go back.'

'I know, Robbie.'

'We'll have to follow this up.'

'Good idea, Robbie.'

We began to climb. The shaft started to level after a few minutes, like we were going up one side of a huge arch. There were welding splotches everywhere and the lines of rivets were uneven and straggly. Yoona noticed it too.

'Whoever built this was in a hurry.'

I remembered those pale faces streaming with rainwater, the children staggering under loads of plate-glass. Yes, Yoona, they were in a hurry.

'I was sick through most of my prex, Robbie. You haven't

told me what you saw there. On Py-Two.'

She paused a moment and looked down. It was a crazy thing to be talking about in the middle of an airshaft and going nowhere we knew. But everything was crazy now.

'They were taking the pyramid apart to build Deepwater. Hundreds of people, all colours, all in a hurry. And there was another pyramid city in the distance—'

'Py-One.' Her voice was a whisper above the hiss of air. The shaft was lighter now and nearly level.

'That had been taken apart, too. Nearly all of it was gone.'

'The Deepwater before us,' said Yoona in the same low voice. She stopped and we rested. She looked back again.

'Robbie, what did my parents look like? I was sick in the prex and couldn't see things clearly.'

'They both looked like you, Yoona. Your father had fair hair and your mother was red. They were really upset. They must have loved you.'

Yoona didn't say anything. She just lay there in the shaft ahead of me, her head pillowed in her arms. I knew she was crying and I knew she didn't want me to see. Her shoulders shook once, just for a moment. Then she raised her head again.

'Thanks, Robbie.'

She set off again and I followed. Yoona never asked me about her parents again.

There was another of those circular airlock covers ahead. We wriggled through and it clicked shut behind us like the other one. It was a nasty, final little sound.

Now the shaft was branching in all directions, like a maze. Yoona kept going, following the dim light, down a shaft, sideways, then up and level again. And the little airlock traps clicked shut like jaws snapping. We were crawling through the spaceship like ants lost in an ocean liner; I felt a thrill of horror, remembering how long Deepwater was. We could crawl like this forever.

Well . . . not forever.

Then Yoona stopped. She looked back and made herself

speak as calmly as she could. 'Robbie, we're at a dead end.'

There was enough light ahead to see the blank metal wall. One of those little traps had just clicked shut behind us. That meant our coffin was about ten metres long, a metre high and a metre wide. Even as I thought that, I didn't believe it. Being so close in this spaceship, or maybe being in that prex, had done something to me. The people who built this ship didn't want anyone to die in it. I could sense it as clearly as if they'd hammered the message into the metal.

'There's light, Yoona, It must be coming from somewhere.'

She looked back and tried to smile.

'Is that Reb speaking?'

'No, it's the Earthkid, Robbie Mikkelson.'

There was nothing to be funny about. But we did laugh for a moment although I felt I wanted to cry, too. There were pains up and down my body and my arms and legs hurt every time they moved. Yoona gasped as she laughed – she must have been hurting, too. Then she began to move forwards again, knocking the sides of the tunnel, the floor and ceiling. They sounded solid.

We were at the end now. Yoona banged the last panels and then the blank wall itself. It gave a different sound and she passed her hands over it, straining to see in the dim light.

'Robbie, this wall isn't metal.' Her voice trembled with excitement. 'It's a kind of glass . . . and I've seen it before.'

'Where?'

Yoona didn't answer. She pushed herself up as close as she could to the blank wall and pushed very hard. It must have been another airlock like those circular ones. The 'wall' snapped forwards and Yoona shot through. I grabbed her legs but was pulled after her and we fell into what seemed like a bottomless shaft.

The air was suddenly bright and yellow and we fell . . . but not real falling. The pressure was so dense that we floated down. We could breathe but my ears popped and my heart pounded. Yoona floated ahead, her hair trailing. She even tried to turn and signal to me. She was trying to say something, but the air pressure was too thick.

We fell down and down, arms and legs wide as in one of those free-fall parachute jumps. And instead of falling faster, we went slower as the air pressure thickened like soft yellow cushions. Now we were more like two swimmers, and below I could see a twinkling ocean floor.

We didn't crash on to this floor. We just sank down and at the bottom the air was clear as though above was a kind of forcefield.

The 'ocean floor' was metal, set with hundreds of tiny crystals. Around us were the walls of a small room, plated solid yellow and glowing with energy. Down each side were batteries of huge, glowing consoles.

And we didn't have this room to ourselves. As I picked myself up, something moved. Opposite me, and blinking at us from wide, glittery, black eyes, was a two-legged creature. It was the strangest thing I had ever seen.

'Yoona,' I said. 'Is that NUN?'

17 Where life began

Yoona was picking herself up. The thing made a clattering sound at us, blinking quickly.

'*That* thing!' Then she laughed happily, like she couldn't believe anything.

No, I suppose not. Not unless NUN was about the size of a large chicken with two legs ending in clawed feet, two little claw-handed arms and a body covered with flat, glossy, olive-green feathers. The neck was arched, with a bird-like head, big red crest and sharp, cruel beak.

'Robbie . . .' Yoona was still laughing but it was a funny, breathless laugh. 'That is Zak's compy.'

Then it hit her. We were trapped in this strange little room with a strange little monster and she didn't care at all. She gave me a proper smile, no longer laughing.

'And this is the magic cave.'

The magic cave. NUN's terminal room! Where their unseen super-parent had made all those things for them, so . . . so that little dinosaur . . .

'Is that a solid-hologram?'

'Right, Robbie.' Yoona was examining the controls set round a large door. 'So that means behind this door is . . .' She looked at me and whispered the words in capital letters ' . . . OUR PLACE.'

The place where life began. The fantastic room where they had woken up naked in yellow light. Yoona was as happy and excited as a young kid let loose with a credit card.

'NUN showed us how to set these controls,' she muttered.

117

'Compsognathus . . . Jurassic period . . . I helped Zak work out the coordinates.'

I looked back. The 'compy' made little clutching movements with its claw-hands and the black eyes flashed angrily. It was looking at me like I'd make a nice lunch.

'Yoona, what did those things eat?'

'Solid holograms don't eat, Robbie.' She was still running her hands up and down the controls and muttering to herself.

'Why did Zak want a small dinosaur?' She'd told me, but I couldn't remember.

'Because NUN wouldn't make him a big one, Robbie.'

Oh yes, I remembered then. NUN had been making a fresh set of pets and Zak's first choice was a Tyrannosaurus. Which meant we would have been in here with a six-metre high monster. I had another look at the compy.

'It's got feathers.'

'Robbie, some small dinosaurs had feathers, all right? Now let me work this out.' She was passing her hands over the top crystals and began spelling out words as she did. 'I'm sure it could be opened from this side as well.'

I hoped so. Otherwise we could be here a very long time and the solid-hologram compy might decide it was hungry after all. Yoona made to press the centre crystal, then she stopped and looked at me. I think it really sank in then – she was going back to where she began. Her lips trembled, then she set them in a firm line and pressed the centre crystal.

The door slid apart in two sections and suddenly it was like looking into the sun. The light in here was golden, but nothing like the intense brilliance that flooded in, so thick and warm that it was like standing in hot water.

The compy ducked out before us and ran twittering into the glow. Yoona stood there and let it blaze like yellow fire on her body. She put out her hand and I took it. She tugged, come on, and we went out into the chamber of NUN.

It was the same shape and size as the room on the other ship. But different, the way a black-and-white photo is different

118

from the real thing. The walls seemed to jet up into the ceiling like rockets of dazzling light. And in the centre, suspended by itself, was a globe of yellow energy. It seemed the size of a basketball but must have been much bigger. And even to call it yellow or golden was wrong because it glowed and shone like someone had taken a spoonful of pure sunlight and patted it into a ball, then let it hover by itself. As I watched, a faint humming seemed to start in the sun-ball and something tingled over us like an invisible hand.

A long drape by the terminal door flashed and glowed with a hundred incredible patterns. 'Silk from the Martian rainbow-bug,' said Yoona softly and passed her hand across it. The folds shone with living colour.

I wasn't really listening. I was looking around and couldn't believe anything was really like this. The floor was golden and spread with dozens of brightly-coloured rugs that tumbled over each other like waves. There were stacks of equipment that looked like giant stereos, but nobody on Deepwater had even mentioned the word 'music'. There were clothes, jewellery and paintings like the slides Ms Booth showed us on famous art. A Roman statue with a huge straw hat on its head. And everything thrown everywhere, the way kids do in their room.

There was stuff that must have come from the Martian colonies – flowers of all crazy shapes and colours in silver pots, even one of those spike-plant things I'd seen near Py-Two. Hologram butterflies and a strange little flying snake with bat wings that flashed bright green flitted among them.

Yoona knew all their names, even the little snake, a Martian bat-viper. She was walking and turning round, tripping over the clutter and not caring. She kicked over a glittering hooded suit made out of little metal scales – armour for hunting Martian ice-worms, she said. Then I froze as a voice overhead called Yoona's name.

'Yoo-na . . . Yoo-na,' it squawked.

Down out of the golden heaven flapped a big bird, patched with red, yellow, blue and green. Yoona's parrot.

'Splotchy!' Her face lit up like Christmas as it landed on her shoulder. 'I called it that because it was all splotched with colour.' She ran her hands down the glossy feathers and it nibbled her ear. She whispered to it and grinned at me. 'I never thought I'd see Splotchy again.'

The whole room had just about knocked me over. But seeing her parrot up close made me start to think. The 'live' holograms weren't as real as the objects. There were tiny dots glowing through them like a video picture up close. Not even NUN could make life real – and anyway, everything here was make-believe.

'Yoona, it's like one of those fantastic hi-tech expo shows . . . but a million times better.'

She nodded and grinned again, tickling the parrot. So I felt really mean when I went on speaking. 'But it's not real, is it? It's . . . I suppose it's like standing in a video game.'

'So?' She giggled. 'Robbie, this is just like I remember it. Look at this—'

She broke off and gave a set of very high whistle-squeaks. From somewhere in the golden haze they were answered and a strange little creature hopped up and blinked big saucer-eyes at us. It was pear-shaped, covered with blue fur, and had fan-like ears, one large paddle-foot and a long tail. It squeaked again and wound the tail round its body.

'Lis's sand-diver.' Yoona giggled again. It was a silly giggle and didn't sound like her. 'Anything like this on Planet Earth, Robbie?'

'Yoona, they're not real.'

'They're real enough for me, Robbie. Anyway, don't you feel great?'

Yes, I was feeling better. The humming from that sun-ball was a bit louder and the golden light seemed to go right through my body, wiping away all the aches and pains. Yoona gave a long, happy sigh and gently shooed her parrot away a moment. She began to unzip her tunic.

'We don't need clothes in here, Robbie, not this stuff anyway.'

'Ah, Yoona—' I stopped her just in time. 'Could you keep them on till – till I get used to it?'

'OK, Robbie-Wobbie.'

Robbie who? Yoona just gave a big grin and let herself fall back on to a couch, eyes shut, arms and legs spread wide like she was sunbathing. Then I realised what was wrong.

My dad doesn't drink much, but a couple of nights after he got fired he came home really floating. Yoona was floating, too, but on this golden atmosphere. She was a kid again, back in her golden NUN-place and as high as a kite.

'Yoona, shall we look around?'

'You look around, Robbie-Wobbie.'

'All right then, I will, Yoony-Boony.'

She just gave another long giggle. I was starting to get a funny lightness in my head now. I did look around and made myself think – think about the first time Yoona had talked about NUN, after my second prex while we sat at the controls of Deepwater.

There were two doors in this place, she had said. One led to the main deck, the second was the NUN door at the other end. Yoona lay there without moving, the parrot back on her shoulder. She was singing to herself. I turned and began walking down the huge golden room.

Every step of the way there was something. Sports gear and hi-tech stuff I'd never seen, even six thrones in a circle, one with a china bunny on it. On the floor were dozens of big, round jewels that shone like blue fire. Jupiter moonstones, Yoona had said; miners could dig all their lives and not find one. These were lying round here in their dozens and I kicked them aside like basketballs. I was really light-headed now and the room hummed round me like a golden powerhouse.

The end wall was a massive long stretch of butter yellow. In the centre was an arch, draped with rainbow silk. It was about four metres high by two metres wide and ended in a sharp point. I pulled down the silk and there behind it was the NUN door.

Yoona had described that door – cut from a solid slab of Martian rain-crystal, like cloudy glass with tiny, bright sparkles of light. The glass was like that last barrier before we fell into the terminal. But behind this door the yellow light had shone even more brightly, as though it led into the golden sun-heart of NUN.

It was still shining through the crystal like a sun through water. But at the bottom, a dark-red line had appeared and was starting to slowly fill like blood dripping into a glass. It made me sick just to look at it.

Jel.

I backed away. That crystal door looked super-strong, but jel at full strength could force anything. And although it was filling slowly, there was no reason to hang around. I was almost relieved to see it because jel would snap Yoona out of her trip quicker than anything.

The humming behind me was louder and I looked up. The sun-ball flashed so brightly that I was dazzled and there was a high-pitched yowl for a moment, like static. My ears buzzed a little and I could hear Yoona singing somewhere. Time to get out of here.

I started walking quickly back. The light was heavy and wrapped round me like a thick yellow blanket. Ahead was something like furniture, draped with the rainbow silk. My foot caught as I went past and pulled the drape off. Underneath was more rain-crystal, but in a long coffin shape that I knew at once. That line of black, oblong shapes on the other Deepwater. These were the ones Yoona and the others had woken up inside.

I pulled the rest of the silk off. There were eight caskets here, but only six on the other ship. Why? The first six of them were empty, but through the crystal I could see padded couches like the insides of coffins. It made me shudder because my body – Reb – had lain in one of those.

The two at the end were closed and dark. I tried to look in one and suddenly noticed something. Everywhere had gone very quiet. Then the dark crystal blazed with reflected light as the sun-ball shone so brightly it filled the room with fire. And from overhead, a voice spoke my name.

'Robbie?'

Not a human voice, not even a machine or solid-hologram. It seemed to be shaped out of that golden yellow light and I had never heard anything like it before. But I knew who it was. NUN.

'Yes?' I said.

'Speak my name, Robbie.' The voice was talking to me like a favourite uncle I hadn't seen for years.

'You're NUN.' There was no answer but the light blazed very hotly again for a moment. 'How do you know my – my Earth name.'

'You were mine, Robbie.'

'Reb was yours, not me.' This was unreal, talking to someone I couldn't see. 'Look, I have to get back to Yoona, the jel—'

'What is jel, Robbie?'

NUN didn't know what jel was? An alarm-bell should have gone off then. I should have worked something out and then – then something really bad might not have happened. I didn't though, and the golden light was drowning me.

'The stuff behind the door, it's—'

'I won't let it hurt you, Robbie.'

And it was still unreal because the golden voice seemed amused by what I said, as though I'd just used another name for something it knew about. My head felt hot – I was flushed and sleepy. NUN's voice, the power of this room, were filling me with gooey, yellow treacle, slowing me down, stopping me.

'Yoona,' I said. I had to think for a moment who she was.

'Go to Yoona.'

Yoona had started to sing again, somewhere in the golden haze. I began walking towards her, my feet catching and tripping on stuff. NUN was silent but the light was strong and golden – I knew I was being watched. Then a boot landed on the floor in front of me.

'Hi, Wobbie-boy!'

Yoona was sitting up on her couch, fitting a silver slipper on her foot. She had one of those old-fashioned black top hats on her head, with big ostrich feathers stuck in it. She had rings on all her fingers and a long flute tucked in her tunic pocket.

'Hey, listen!' She played some notes on the flute then gave me a big stupid grin. 'Not bad, eh?'

'Yoona, there's jel behind that crystal door and NUN—'

'Door's extremely thick, 'sides NUN'll look after us, told me.' She gave a sleepy wave upward. 'NUN says not to worry about anything-thing-ting.'

'What do you mean?'

I was getting a horrible feeling. Above and round us, the golden light shimmered and although NUN hadn't spoken, I knew it was listening and I got that sense again, of being laughed at. Yoona was pulling off her other boot and pulling on the silver slipper.

' 'Cos we're staying here, Wobsie . . . NUN says we can . . . not worry about anything for ever and ever, ever, ever . . . found us again . . . very happy.'

NUN had found us again. And this time NUN would not let us go.

18   The golden toyland

We were going to stay here. NUN had been talking to Yoona,
too. It did seem wonderful, but I knew it wasn't right. Not
right because of Yoona putting on the slipper and kicking her
other boot away. And with all that crazy gear on.

I knew Yoona by now. I'd seen her at the controls of
Deepwater, fighting the ameb. I'd seen her so tired she couldn't
stand, but still fighting. And she nearly lost her own life helping
me on the other Deepwater.

Deepwater was where she belonged. It was full of danger, bare
metal walls and decks, fighting, bickering kids, but it was her
spaceship and this golden place wasn't part of her life. NUN was
trying to pull her back to it and NUN controlled this place.

'Yoona,' I whispered, 'do you want to stay here?'

She blinked at me like I'd said something very stupid.

'Wobsie, NUN wants me to stay.'

I was kneeling beside her. I had an idea and felt like a rat
for taking advantage of her, but I had to.

'And what about the other NUN ... on the other
Deepwater ... ?'

'All power gone, poor thing, too long alone ... could
scarcely talk.' Her eyes were half-closed and she might have
been talking about the weather, she was so casual. 'Tried to
tell me about ... about keeping alive ... everything left on
our ship, had to always go on ... go on ...'

'Go on where?'

'There ... circle on door.' The NUN circle? What did she
mean?

'What else did that NUN say?'

'Wobbie-wobbie, don't want to talk about it, too sad.' She laughed and got up. 'Show you my Pwincess Di Wedding Dwess, that's a weal scweam, Wobbie-Wobbie!'

She burst out laughing like it was the funniest joke ever and her parrot squawked. Somewhere in the golden haze the compy squeaked, and there was a ripping sound as a length of rainbow silk floated to the ground.

'Yoona . . . those two closed coff – caskets . . .'

I'd nearly said 'coffins', the ones on the other Deepwater that she hadn't let me near. I remember her torch flashing down and her fierce gesture – stay back!

'What was in them? Please tell me.'

'Us, Robbie. We were in them.'

Yoona opened her eyes wide and the smile went for a moment. The horror of that memory almost broke the golden spell. She went on in the same faraway voice, the parrot fluttering overhead and the sand-diver bouncing and squeaking like a rubber cushion.

'Us. We were in those caskets but as adults, grown up . . . and . . . and sleeping. Now the adult-us is gone.' She blinked sleepily. 'Wanna sleep now, tired.'

Us. Yoona and me as adults. Those drifting white space suits on the upper deck with the other kids' names on them. They were adult-size, too. No wonder Yoona looked so bad when the spaceship was being destroyed. No wonder she prexed, knowing what she did. The whole thing, all the mystery, was getting worse and we had to get *out*.

'Yoona,' I whispered as low as I could, my lips against her ear. 'We have to get out of here, see the others.'

'Don't want them . . .' Then she muttered something about that rockhead Jupie and his sandbrain girlfriend. 'They're all silly-sil-sil . . .' She tried to lie back but I hooked her arm over my shoulder and pulled her up.

'Let's get back to the control deck.'

'No!' She resisted and she was strong.

'No, Robbie,' came the golden tones from overhead.

Yoona looked up like a hopeful kid when Mum or Dad are handing out dollars. 'NUN, don't want to go,' she said, like not wanting to go to bed. 'You must stay, Robbie.'

The golden light blazed and burned inside me as though I was being melted. There was steel in those golden words. Yoona hung on my shoulder like a dead-weight.

'I can give you everything you want, Robbie. I can make all your dreams. Shall I make your parents for you? Your brother and sister?'

Everything hot inside me went cold with fear at the thought. And I had to be very careful, for NUN seemed to know everything.

'No, NUN, I mean . . . we have to bring the others here. They've forgotten how wonderful everything is, they have to come.'

The light burned like I was being screened for truth. Then NUN spoke again in words of melting gold.

'Go on, Robbie.'

'We'll go together – ah, to the door,' I said loudly and pulled Yoona along. She gave a little squeal of protest. I bent down to grab her boots and we nearly overbalanced. The humming from the sun-ball was louder but uncertain, like bees buzzing. I think NUN was uncertain but wanted all the children back.

A pile of vid-books crashed over. Yoona was still muttering about rockheads and sandbrains, but she let me take her. I booted away a pile of golden crowns and Yoona just hummed, a silly dreamtime look on her face. The parrot flew with us and kept trying to settle on her top-hatted head.

Then we were at the door, set with symbols and that circle which the NUN on the other Deepwater said meant something. What? Yoona giggled, pointing at it. The door didn't have a handle.

'All right, smarty-Wobs, open it.'

'NUN,' I said, looking up at the humming sun-ball. 'How do we open the door?'

I still don't think NUN would have told us, but Yoona saved us without meaning to. She flopped back against the door and shook her head, calling out like she'd just woken up.

'Yeah, yeah, let him go, NUN, I just want to enjoy myself.'

She pushed herself back from the door, her hand flat on the circle. There was a little buzzing click from somewhere and she flinched as if she'd been bitten. Then that solid steel door swung open, light as plastic.

Yoona's hand had unlocked it like a palm-print key. She gaped a moment, then giggled again. 'There you are, Wobsie-Wobsie—'

I ducked my head down and charged forwards, wrapping my arms round her. We both went through the door and crashed in a heap. Yoona's yell mixed with Splotchy's squawk of surprise. At once there was a roar of anger from inside.

'Robbie!'

I scrambled up. A cloud of golden light rushed at me and I kicked the door shut. It slammed, then shook like something punched it.

Yoona was picking herself up. Splotchy had come through as well and was fluttering round her. I put my back against the door.

'Get away,' Yoona said, puzzled, like I'd done something strange.

'No, it's a toyland in there. NUN just wants us back in kindergarten.'

'Robbie, get out of the way!' No more 'Wobbie', she was getting angry now. I got myself ready for the fight.

'Yoona, Bren can't fly Deepwater very long.'

'Get away!' Her eyes were blazing.

'Deepwater, Yoona, Deepwater, it's your spaceship!'

She punched very hard and fast and I was waiting for it. I ducked even faster and her fist hit the circle-symbol on this side of the door. It didn't open – only a palm-print did that – but Yoona really hurt her knuckles. She yelled with pain and I tried to grab her arms.

'Yoona, Deepwater – Deepwater!'

'Don't tell me what to do.' She was trying to break my grip, banging my back against the door. 'I want NUN—'

'Yoona, look at yourself!'

I pushed her back and she staggered. Then she stopped as if I'd slapped her. She must have felt it happening. Her eyes went wide and her hands up to her head. The top hat and feathers were disappearing and the length of rainbow silk faded into nothing. So did the silver slippers from her feet and the flute from her pocket.

Splotchy squawked, too, but in a thin, scratchy way. The parrot was fading; I could see the metal wall of the passage through the red and green wings. Yoona put her hand up and the disappearing bird tried to sit on her finger. It tried to squawk again, but just vanished in a sparkle of tiny dots.

Yoona was left with her hand out, looking at nothing. She was stunned, frowning. I got up and stood against the door again, ready for round two.

But she wasn't angry now. She was looking round, down at her feet then up at me. She blinked as though coming out of a bad dream. I didn't move from the door. Behind it there was no sound.

'Robbie . . . did I hit you?'

'No, you tried to.' Lucky I ducked, because when Yoona hits, you stay flattened.

She took a quick step forward and I jumped a little but she just gave me a tight hug. 'Sorry,' she whispered. There was a tearful eyelash on my cheek.

'Listen, Yoona, we'd better get back.'

'Yes, let's go.' She shuddered a bit and turned.

'Ah – your boots?'

Yoona bent to pull them on. Then she leaned against the wall a moment and I saw the whole weight of Deepwater go back on her shoulders. Without looking at the NUN door, she began walking quickly down the corridor.

I followed. Yoona began to trot. We had nearly been eaten

by jel, nearly sucked into space, crawled through the insides of Deepwater and found a fantasy room where she was born. No wonder it nearly zapped her mind, but now she was Yoona again and Bren was flying her spaceship.

The corridor was made of shining metal and was nearly half a kilometre long. Even the air was different from that golden room. Yoona must have remembered everything.

'I told you about the other NUN, didn't I?' she said suddenly.

'Yes. And now you have to tell the others.'

'I know.' She gave a pale little smile and added, 'Wobbie.' I wished I knew some Martian nicknames.

We reached the end door. Yoona looked at me and pressed her hand into the circle design. Another tiny buzzing click and it opened. So simple, and yet it was another mystery. Why didn't we know about that? Did even NUN know how to open that door? I had a little headache now and I was breathless from that long job, feeling a bit sick. That was a bad sign.

Lis was below deck when we came through. She gasped at us and her loud yell brought Zak and Gret. Up top we could hear Bren shouting instructions for COL to put Deepwater into a holding pattern.

'We thought you were trapped, and we tried to get you out!' Lis's blue skin was very pale. 'That horrible stuff nearly got into the upper deck!'

'We tried to save you.' Gret's voice was cold and bitter, her eyes like green stones.

Zak was limping and so was Gret, one ankle of her track suit torn away. Lis had a sleeve missing and a bandaged arm. When Bren appeared, his tunic was torn across the front and he had red burn-marks on the side of his neck.

No wonder they took so long to open the port and eject the jel! They'd come down into the lower deck as far as they could, lasers blazing, to see if we were still alive, and fought the jel as long as they could. Yoona tried to speak, but Lis squealed again as though she'd suddenly realised.

'And they came back through the NUN door!'

There was silence. Then their faces went open and hopeful, even Gret, like all their troubles were over. I realised how much they'd missed their golden toyland. Even Zak was smiling, for the first time since I'd known him.

'We can't take you there,' said Yoona. 'You'd never come out.'

'We wouldn't want to come out! We were happy there!' yelled Zak.

'You're not our captain any more! You don't tell us what to do!' Gret was shouting now, angry and sharp. 'We decide that!'

'I'm not showing you how to open that door,' yelled Yoona. 'Just let me explain—'

They wouldn't, though. Lis was unhappy and silent. Bren and Yoona were blaming each other and Zak was yelling for the NUN door to be opened.

I wanted to help Yoona, but I was too tired. I couldn't even speak because my head ached like heavy boots were marching through it. And that little buzz behind my eyes was starting. Even before I told myself what it was, I heard Yoona appealing for me to confirm what she said – then Gret, deadly and spiteful: 'Him? He'd say whatever you wanted him to.'

And Zak, still raging about NUN. 'He can't even stop prexing.'

I tried to speak, but the darkness was rushing over. My fifth prex, the bad one. I tried to lift my head up and heard Bren's next words.

'It doesn't matter. We're turning Deepwater round.'

Then everything spun.

19   Prexing out

The darkness sucked over me and the buzzing behind my eyes
became a loud screech. It was like being a small kid out of my
depth in the water. Every time I broke the surface a black hand
pushed me back under. Yoona's hands were shaking me, then
one was resting on my forehead and I heard her say 'Robbie',
then more loudly, 'Robbie!'

I opened my eyes. There was sunlight coming in the window
and the plastic bomber was dangling overhead from the ceiling
of my bedroom. I must have looked really freaked out because
Mum snatched her hand away from my forehead and looked
almost scared.

'Robbie?'

'I'm OK, Mum.' I wasn't, but keeping secrets from adults
means telling lies. 'Bad dream, that's all.'

'Breakfast,' she said. She gave me another worried look
and left.

I got dressed. My clothes felt clumsy and – and out of date,
like clothes out of history. Today . . . the radio in the other
room said today was a bright new Monday. What became of
Sunday? And did my parents know I'd missed a day? I didn't
want to leave the bedroom, but I made myself. The sooner I
went on with this the sooner I'd get back to Deepwater where
everything was real.

If I got back. This was my fifth prex, they always ended
about then, even one as complete as mine. Maybe then
Reb would somehow take over again. But I couldn't let
myself think that, even if I did have a horrible, deep-down

feeling that this was my last prex.

I had to force myself to think about things like school, Meatgrinder, what happened on Saturday, but all of it was nothing – nothing.

But I knew Mum's tactics. She wouldn't talk to me about Saturday and Meatgrinder. She'd talk to the principal and he'd talk to Meatgrinder's mum. Then she'd talk to Meatgrinder, then the principal again, and he'd talk to me and Meatgrinder.

I had breakfast. I had to chew and chew the Earth-food before I could swallow it. And I kept thinking about Sunday, which didn't exist for me. But how do you say, hey Mum and Dad, I spent a lot of the weekend locked in the lower deck of a spaceship with a side-trip to Mars? It was all so crazy I nearly cried.

'You've got that science lab thing today, haven't you, son?' Dad asked.

'Yeah, Dad, then hockey practice.' I'd nearly forgotten what hockey was!

'So you'll be home by five,' said Mum in a voice that meant *be* home by five.

'Yes, Mum.'

'You're lucky to have a friend like Denie,' she said in a voice that meant I was *very* lucky.

'Yes, Mum.' What had Denie done for me?

'And try and stay out of Connal's way until this is sorted.'

'Yes, Mum.' I always tried to stay out of Connal's way.

'And Connal has been told to stay out of yours.'

Yes, Dad, he'd wait until my back was turned. I grabbed my lunch and headed for the door. Then I turned. They were sitting there looking at me and just for a moment, their outlines flickered and froze like a video still.

'Just hang loose, kiddo.'

'I'll hang loose, Mum.'

I wanted to go back and put my arms round them and be hugged and forget the bad dreams. But I couldn't because this was a bad dream and Deepwater was the reality. I shut the door, feeling sick. My stomach wasn't used to Earth-food any more. And that unreal feeling got worse as I cycled slowly down the drive. At the bottom, Denie Miles was waiting on her bike.

'I'm back,' I said. 'I'm Robbie. Did you get me home?'

She nodded. 'I came back into the room to check before I phoned.' She looked at me carefully. 'You're a lot quieter after you prex.'

'Quiet . . . how quiet?'

Denie cycled a moment, thinking. 'Total bore,' she said, and smiled.

She'd just found me sitting on the bed, silent. So she took me home and pushed me through my bedroom window. When my folks found me, they put me to bed. Denie phoned them to say I was really worried with a homework assignment and she was helping. Mum and Dad actually thanked her. Then when she saw me on Sunday, I was a hundred per cent normal Robbie. There was no sign of Reb, no memory of Deepwater.

'You believe me,' I said.

'Yes,' she said. 'I really don't know why, Robbie.' She put a hand over her stomach. 'I just have a feeling here. A strange feeling . . .'

It was a few minutes to school-time, so we swung our bikes off to one side. Denie was thinking very hard. 'You prex back much earlier than the others. But didn't Yoona say you look like a South Martian?'

'Yes.'

'So that means Reb is an extension of you.' Then she asked suddenly, 'Hey, do they know about sex?'

'Sex?'

'Yes, they're teenagers.'

'Sorry, Denie, I forgot to ask them.' I was getting a strange feeling now – about Denie.

She saw my look and nudged me impatiently. 'Then chemistry, biology, genes, things like that. Come on, think!'

I did and shook my head. 'They never mentioned them.'

'But those symbols in the NUN circle? I think they're just symbols like artwork, saying something very basic.' She leaned on her handlebars, thinking. 'I have a feeling NUN was very selective in what it taught them.'

'What do they stand for?'

'Earth, fire, water and air. And that means life. So the circle encloses life – or helps it somehow? And the word NUN . . .'

'What?'

'Dad took me to the university library on Sunday. NUN is an Old Testament word from the Bible. It was a very early name and it also meant "fish". She was frowning, not sure of herself. 'And a fish could be a symbol of life: reproduction.'

More kids were biking to school, Reeboks with them. I saw his head turn, which meant trouble as soon as he saw Meatgrinder.

'And what does the circle mean?'

Denie sighed. 'I don't know – everything goes in a circle, doesn't it? That's the theory.'

'The universe doesn't. It just goes on forever.'

'No Robbie, the universe does go in a circle.' Suddenly it was like a lot of thoughts were slotting together. 'Maybe that's it, the circle of the universe.'

She banged her hands on the handlebars of her bike in frustration. 'Oh hell, Robbie, why can't *I* be on that spaceship? What an incredible, mind-blowing thing to happen – and *why* is it there?'

'Why?'

'Yes – why?' It wasn't just built for six kids, that whole third section. What's in there?'

'We can't get to it.'

'You should try! There must be something in that third section, not just the power plant but something so important that they took their cities apart for it.'

She glared at me with excitement and tension. It was like Denie had suddenly just realised how awesome all this was. Then the school bell rang.

I swung my bike round. 'Let's go somewhere and keep talking.'

'No.' She grabbed my handlebars. 'Let's just go through like a normal day. Something's going to happen, Robbie, something will click.'

'How do you know?'

'You didn't freak out when you ended up on Deepwater, because you had a feeling it was right. Well, I've got a feeling, Robbie—'

She stopped, looking at me, her lips tight. I nodded and she grinned. 'Come on, we'll be late.'

We went to where the others were waiting. I must have looked funny, because Ms Booth asked me if I was all right.

'You won't be all right when I get you,' breathed Meatgrinder in my ear. He'd already conned himself into believing that Saturday was an accident.

She gave us a little lecture while we waited for the bus. About science, birth and our bodies, genetic selection and how anybody who made trouble would get extra-heavy trouble right back. Then the bus came and we got in.

Glyn Evans was going to sit beside me, but Denie elbowed him aside. Ms Booth made Meatgrinder sit in the front. I was starting to feel bad again and Denie nudged me.

'Are you OK?'

I nodded. But I wasn't, I knew I was going to prex and I *couldn't*, not until I got some answers. My head started to spin and I tried to reverse the spin direction. The bus engine roared round me and everything, even Denie, flickered like video pictures. Denie knew something was very wrong and she'd seen me prex before.

'Hang on!' she whispered.

She nudged me, then jogged me hard. She even jabbed me with a pencil and somehow the spin slowed down. All the picture-flickering stopped – but it was waiting to start up again. I made myself think, ask questions.

'Prexing,' I muttered.

'What about it?'

'Why does it happen?' My voice sounded thick and scratchy.

'Don't know, Robbie.'

'Couldn't talk to anyone in Yoona's prex, they couldn't see me.' My words seemed to be pulling out like a tape when the batteries are running down. 'But I can talk to you.'

'This is your prex, not hers, and you can control it.' She jabbed me with the pencil again. 'We're here.'

'What's so important about this place?' I muttered.

'Genes, reproduction, life, NUN the fish – and the end of your prex cycle, remember?' She nudged me again. 'There must be something here.'

I must have looked terrible getting off the bus because Ms Booth again asked me if I was all right.

I didn't care about anything any more. My head was going like a slow-grinding blender, my eyes were blurred and things kept flashing. I wanted to lie down and go to sleep.

We were being taken into a long, white-painted room where someone in a white coat showed us things and talked about biology. I could hardly make sense of what she said.

'A gene sample can come from a hair, a trace of blood, a bone sample,' said the woman, 'I suppose you all know the biblical story of Eve being made from Adam's rib.'

'Only proves the Bible was written by men,' muttered Ms Booth and Denie gave a 'right on' under her breath.

Now the woman was talking about genes and selective breeding. She had dark hair and a nice grin and made it all sound really interesting. Cloning from a gene was like getting hundreds of prints from one negative and you could get a gene from just about anywhere on the body. 'Pardon me,' she said, and pulled out a hair on Meatgrinder's head. He yelped and scowled as everyone laughed. Then she did the same with Denie, 'gene cells are everywhere', and Denie gasped too, but not because of the hair. She began to whisper something and that was when Meatgrinder kicked me very hard.

He'd been lining up and waiting until Ms Booth wasn't

looking. His boot hit me right at the base of my back. I turned round, a bolt of Deepwater's energy exploding in me, and punched him right in the middle of his fat, sneering face.

Everything hung out. The whole class came apart round us as Meatgrinder and I rolled together on the floor, trying to land as many punches as we could. All the kids were yelling. Ms Booth was yelling, too, and trying to pull us apart. Meatgrinder landed one on my nose and I got one back, bang on his fat lips. Then the dark-haired woman stepped in between us, speaking cheerfully like we were specimens in a bottle.

'Good example,' she said. 'Animals go through involved mating rituals so the female can select the best male. In this case, two boys—'

A little silver thing flashed in front of my eyes. I made to pull back, but Denie grabbed my wrist. 'Let her do it,' she whispered, and I froze. The woman drew the spoon away with a tiny speck of blood on it.

'That's all I need,' she said and gave me that nice smile. 'In a sense now, you might live again.'

Then something funny happened. She looked at me and Denie and it was like something froze between us. Then she blinked and slipped the spoon into a white box.

Ms Booth was pulling Meatgrinder and me apart. She has eyes in the back of her head and saw everything. Meatgrinder was in real trouble. Denie was pulling me back.

'I'll take Robbie outside,' she said.

The black-haired woman was still watching, a curious look on her face now. Denie took me out, down the corridor and round the side of the building. The sunlight made my eyes water and seemed to burn my skin. I had never felt this bad before and my head was pounding like a rock band.

'Robbie, that was it, that was why you ended up on the spaceship. Your gene.'

'She won't keep it,' I whispered. Denie's face was slipping out of focus.

139

'I'll ask her to, tell her to!' Denie was holding me tight as if I wanted to get away. She shoved the paper with the circle on it under my nose. 'Remember, the genes, cloning, the universe goes in a circle – Robbie!'

Her voice ended on a flickering note like a tape had stopped. Beside her, the air seemed to slit open like two flaps of a tent and Yoona was there.

'Robbie, do you want to come back to Deepwater?'

'Yes.'

Then the tape began running again. Denie was looking at me and I could hear Ms Booth calling us both. Denie's eyes were wide.

'Is she there – Yoona?'

I nodded. 'Yes.' Not yes to Denie, to Yoona. And I heard Yoona speak again.

'Hold tight.'

She was there, her mouth set in a tight line. She punched something into my arm and it was a replay of the first time, the million bright colours.

Denie was stepping back. Or I was and there was someone beside Denie, just like me. Then they freeze-framed and everything came down screaming round like a black whirlpool. I did that awful crash back on to the ground, Yoona holding me tightly. But it was a narrow bed and I opened my eyes in the lower deck of Deepwater.

And this time it was like coming home.

'Welcome back, Robbie.' Yoona grinned with relief and slipped off her headband.

She pulled mine off. I sat up. My head was still spinning, but this time it seemed final. Everything on Planet Earth was unreal, belonging to another Robbie across time and space. Deepwater was my spaceship and Yoona was my captain.

'I had to come into your prex. You were getting bad.'

'My prex cycle was finishing. You might have got Reb back.'

She smiled again. 'I think I got you both.'

Then I realised we weren't alone. Gret and Lis were there

140

with us. Gret was still scowling, but Lis tried a little smile. The hatch was closed.

'Yoona, why are they down here?'

'Bren doesn't want us on deck,' said Yoona. 'He and Zak are running Deepwater.'

'Yoona told us what happened in the NUN chamber,' said Lis. She looked at Gret. 'We believed her, but all Bren can think about is being commander.'

'And Zak thinks if we turn round, NUN will look after us again,' said Yoona.

'Turn Deepwater round?'

'Bren and Zak have used COL to keep the access hatch to the upper deck shut. Nobody gets on the upper deck unless they say so.' Yoona sounded more despairing than I'd ever seen her.

'Nobody gets up there?' I said.

'You catch on quick, Earthkid.' Gret gave an impatient hiss, her eyes as cold and dark as seawater. 'We're all prisoners now.'

20   Outside into horror

Yoona pushed me into one of the shower-licks first. I was wet and dry in ten seconds again, clothes and all. Then she made me drink something and eat a biscuit.

Lis and Gret realised it was too dangerous to go back into the NUN chamber. Maybe even Bren did too, but Yoona was challenging his new authority and he was on the biggest power trip of all time. And Zak was pushing him on like Reeboks with Meatgrinder. All Zak could think about was getting back into the NUN chamber.

The shouting ended when they shut and locked the upper hatch. They had left the intercom open and were scanning for jel. But we weren't allowed out until they had reprogrammed the guidance systems and set new courses.

'Cloning,' said Yoona. 'That would explain us.'

She was walking up and down. Gret was sitting on the steps and Lis lying on her bed, staring at the ceiling. Gret looked at Yoona, then at me.

'We were cloned from gene cells? By NUN?'

'It makes sense,' I said. 'NUN must be a reproduction unit, programmed to do it at the right time.'

'*What* right time?' Gret wasn't near believing it.

'The right time to fly the spaceship.' Yoona was speaking in a low, certain voice as though a memory time lock had opened. 'The people who made Deepwater were sending it somewhere. Even past the known star positions, COL could automatically pilot the ship just on programming. And fly by time-blinking. But Colour-space was different . . .'

Deepwater would need humans hands to guide it through the jungle of dangers like trites, amebs, even mag-mets.

'Somebody would have to fly the ship,' said Lis softly.

'Us kids?' said Gret. I think she wanted to believe. 'We had no memory. We had to *learn* to fly Deepwater.'

'Maybe NUN didn't get time to teach us.' Lis kicked her legs and sat up.

I remembered what Denie had said about NUN being selective. 'If NUN wasn't telling us everything, maybe that was monitored – by COL perhaps – and . . .' I remembered Yoona's dream of 'running in terror' the day they woke up below deck. 'Maybe an automatic override went into gear and we were got out.'

'Through a door only we could open, a subconscious program,' said Yoona. Then she smiled at me. 'First time you've said "us", Robbie.'

And there was something else Denie had said. 'The third part of the spaceship that we don't know anything about. Maybe that's the secret of Deepwater.'

'You don't know Deepwater *has* a secret!' snapped Gret.

'It must have. We're going somewhere for a reason.' I swallowed the rest of my biscuit. 'We have to find out what it is.'

'How do we get through NUN – and the jel?' asked Gret. 'You won't even tell us how to get to NUN.'

Yoona glared. I could see trouble coming. Then Lis yelled.

'Vents!' She got off her bed. 'The time Reb and I repaired that meteor-strike in the OMA. Remember, Reb?'

'No, *Robbie* doesn't,' Gret said nastily.

Lis ignored her. 'There were big vents near the tail. Reb – I mean you thought we could open them from the outside.'

'And meet jel coming the other way,' said Gret. I'd thought of that too.

'We can try,' said Yoona.

The OMAs were sealed, so we'd need Bren and COL to get them out. Yoona was already at the intercom, but the conversation lasted about ten seconds. Bren said there'd be no talking until she opened the NUN door. The intercom clicked off and Yoona slammed her hand against the wall, muttering something about rockhead Jupies.

'You could always go out in your space suit,' said Gret sarcastically. Yoona crossed to the locker and began pulling hers out. Gret yelled in a changed tone, 'Hey, I didn't mean that.'

'Can you think of another way?' snapped Yoona in her 'made up my mind' tone of voice.

'Deepwater's moving,' said Lis, 'Yoona, you can't.'

'Moving slowly,' said Yoona, 'there's no danger. Not even Bren would leave me out there.'

I was scared again and I think my legs moved by themselves. I went over and took out my suit. Yoona looked at me then continued dressing.

'You're both crazy!' yelled Gret.

'Deepwater is on this course for a reason,' said Yoona in a low voice. 'It's going somewhere and Bren wants to turn it round. Now we need answers and we need them *before* he does it and wipes the real course!'

She stopped, tensed, then yelled with real anger at the top of her voice. 'This is *my* ship and I'm not going to let him do that!'

Yoona was bonded to Deepwater in a way that none of us were. But right then we all realised it. Gret just looked at Yoona. Then she came over and began taking out her space suit.

'It doesn't need three of us,' said Yoona tensely. Gret ignored her and started dressing. Then Lis went over to her locker.

'Lis, one of us must stay here by the intercom.'

'And it has to be a stupid sandbrain?' said Lis stiffly. North Martians have long memories for insults.

'I'm sorry I called you that.'

There was nothing to joke about right now, but I couldn't resist it. 'Yes, because they don't use South Martian nicknames at all, Yoona.'

She shot me a 'shut up' look, but it was too late.

'You mean like Py-poppies or marsh-hoppers,' said Lis, her smile wicked. 'Wetheads, puddle-bunnies?'

Even Gret nearly smiled. Yoona was putting on her helmet and ignored us. Gret put hers on and said abruptly to me, 'You shouldn't come. You can't remember anything.'

'I want to.'

She gave me another of her cold sea-green looks. Gret hated showing emotions, but I think she did care about my safety. Maybe she even respected me a little now. And I knew she was furious with herself for losing control of Bren.

We clanged over to the airlock where Yoona was already standing. Lis's smile went and suddenly she looked lonely and unhappy. 'Won't COL tell Bren the airlocks are opening?' she asked.

Yoona shook her helmeted head. 'We'll close and seal each one as we go through.'

'Good luck, all of you.'

Lis came up and kissed each one of us. It was a really nice kiss, but there were tears in her eyes. Then we shut and sealed our visors and went into the first airlock. Lis stood there, still unhappy, one hand raised in farewell as the door slid shut.

We sealed the airlock and went through to the next. And the next and the next, without speaking. Then we were in the main port and still nobody spoke. Yoona just walked over and punched the manual control. The huge, black circle of space appeared, as big as a warehouse door.

We stood looking at it for a moment. It was deep, pure black space with almost no trace of colour, just a long shoal of orange lights twinkling in the far distance. Bren had chosen his gulf well. Without looking back, Yoona walked out into the black nothing.

There was a trick to leaving the port on two legs. Those little Reb-echoes were getting few and far between, but one of them saved me. I put my gloved hand on the side and swung myself out. I floated a moment as the weightless hand of deep space picked me up gently, then my boots clanged on the silver-plate skin of Deepwater and I stood upright.

Not upright, but sideways, for sideways was level if you know what I mean. Outside Deepwater there was no up or down, just a huge, black bowl of nothing all round us. I could feel the coldness already and all I could hear was my breathing. There was to be no intercom talking in case Bren or Zak heard us. We linked hands and our metal shoes began clanging silently down the silver-glass side of Deepwater.

It stretched ahead of us like a motorway without end. I remembered those silver-glass plates from Mars. They seemed a mix of glass and metal; they let in energy and kept out radiation, Yoona said. They had glistened smoothly on the sides of the pyramids, but here they were battered and scratched. The lines that joined them were uneven and lumpy as though that was done in a hurry, too. Some of them were starred and cracked by meteor strikes and there were trite drill-marks everywhere, like thousands of tiny moon-craters. But the plated skin of Deepwater was super-hard.

On and on we marched and the silver-glass motorway still stretched endlessly ahead. There was just blackness and silence and the strange, unreal feeling that we were marching into nowhere. We held each other tightly and looked straight ahead. I could hear my breathing more loudly and my legs began to ache. Now there was dust, and tiny rock fragments, underfoot, like a stretch of sandy beach where the dust from an exploded mag-met had glued itself to the silver-plate.

Yoona stopped a moment to let us reclasp hands more firmly. I was looking down at one of the plates. There were words scratched in the surface, capital-letter words like graffiti. They must have been done with a diamond or something. I read them and I felt a chill colder than deep space. I opened my mouth to tell Yoona, but remembered the intercom. I pulled my hand free and pointed down. Just as she looked, it happened.

Deepwater was a well-programmed spaceship and sometimes made minor course alterations by itself. It made one now, to avoid a large chunk of space-rock sailing past. Up it went, just a little – up from level course, that is. Sideways from course or even down, we could have hung on. But the sudden little upward jar jerked our magnetic shoes clear and suddenly the side of Deepwater was skimming past beneath us.

We rolled over, trying to grab at the sides without our space suits ripping on the razor-sharp plate edgings. The giant, black, hungry nothing of space was all round. Now the vents were up to us, then they slipped past and were gone.

Yelling for Bren wouldn't help. One wrong movement of Deepwater and the plates would cut us to pieces. Some of them jutted out a little and we tried to grab them. I got one and so did Gret. We hung on, gasping into our helmets. Yoona grabbed one too and hung on for a moment until her gloved hands slipped. We were too far down the side now ... there was nothing left for her to hang on to except the long streamlined fins set round the huge exhaust.

It was the worst moment of my life. Yoona was so utterly helpless that I felt panic slap me in the face. Then I felt the Reb-echo, as strong as the first prex. The valve for the air-tank – it's a jet-bottle, so use it! The little control-valve was set in the chest of my suit. I flipped it open and plugged my finger over the hissing air to control the flow. Gret's helmeted head was turning towards me.

Like an invisible rod, the jet-bottle pushed me off the side of Deepwater. But I was thinking, Reb was thinking. I jammed it, tried to turn my body and opened it again. This time I jetted down the side, faster, towards Yoona.

She was still fighting. As the big tail fins came up and whisked past, she clutched one and held tight. But she was going too fast and her gloved hands were sliding down the smooth metal edge to the point. Yoona was off the end of the fin as I clutched her wrist and grabbed the tail fin myself. But that meant no finger on the valve and the air was hissing out. I had less than a minute before it all went. I held on to Yoona and my face-mask rubbed the fin. The big, round tunnel of

Deepwater's exhaust was above us. At the end of that tunnel, a huge eyelid seemed to open and close. And a lot closer was something more horrible.

On the rim of the exhaust a trite was perched, looking at us.

Then the hungry eyes came out on stalks, the extra legs grew and the beetle wings spread. It sprang forwards like a nightmare, on to my mask. A long drill-sting grew out of the grey-ribbed belly like a silver needle, straight at my eyes. Just as it touched the iron-glass of my mask, a gloved hand came out of nowhere and knocked it away.

Gret had sped down after me, using her air-tank the way I had, in time to knock the trite sideways. And that meant the thing went for her. Hovering in mid-air, the stalk-eyes swivelled over and it pounced. In the same moment, my hand slipped off the fin and Gret grabbed my wrist. She was holding on to the fin with her other hand. The trite sprang on to her face-mask, drill-sting already growing again.

Gret was holding on to me. Her own hand was about to slip off the fin. I was holding on to Yoona and behind her was the empty blackness of space. The trite was arching, balancing on Gret's face-mask, ready to drill. To fight it, she would have to let go of Yoona and me.

'Let go of us, Gret,' said Yoona. It was the first time any of us had spoken.

She didn't.

We were trailing like three little action-dolls on the tail of a jet-liner. I was nearly out of oxygen and so was Gret – and the horrible grey insect spread its beetle wings again and began to drill. Gret's hand went tight on mine like a scream of panic but she didn't let go.

'Hang on, Robbie.'

Yoona hadn't stopped thinking. She was on the end of our mad daisy-chain and fumbling with her own air-bottle valve. Oh great, I thought, we'll all be out of air. But Yoona knew what she was doing. She always did.

Above us was the huge exhaust tunnel. While she was

hanging there, Yoona had seen that big eyelid opening and closing at the end of the tunnel. It was the airtight cover that controlled the exhaust. Now, the last of us with any fight, she opened her valve and the jet of air whizzed her up into the exhaust tunnel with enough force to drag me and Gret along.

Gret was screaming now – I knew that, although I couldn't hear her – and as Yoona zoomed past, she let go. I grabbed her arm and pulled her after us. We shot up into the exhaust tunnel. I glimpsed Gret's face twisted in pain, then blood spread inside her visor as the trite drilled through.

We were saved by incredible luck, nothing else. The exhaust cover opened as we banged up against it. A hurricane of exhaust fumes blasted against us, but Yoona grabbed the edge and somehow pulled us after her. I had no air left and was blacking out. We tumbled inside, on to a smooth, rounded metal floor, as the cover began to close again.

Gret was trying to pull the trite from her face-mask. Her helmet was full of blood. The ugly thing grew four extra legs to hang on, then arched its body, ready to lay eggs. The cover was closing and I pushed Gret forwards, her head against the metal edge. The cover shut against the edge, clipping the trite off like a pair of scissors.

Then it clicked shut and we were back in Deepwater.

21 Life store

It was dark and the air was very thin and bad-smelling, but there was some pressure – enough for us to hear Gret screaming inside her helmet. Yoona pushed me aside and unsealed the visor, snapping it open and pulling out the trite-sting with it. Gret's screams stopped abruptly as she fainted.

Yoona slammed herself back against the curved wall. For a moment her body went rigid, then with funny scrabbling movements she began to unseal her visor. I helped her and opened my own. Yoona was pale, gasping and shuddering as in deep shock. I must have looked the same. Even so she was already moving, stabbing a gloved hand up the tunnel. We had to move before that valve opened again and maybe blew us back out into deep space.

We took Gret between us. Her face was covered in blood and it was impossible to tell where the trite-sting had hit her, although I could guess. We dragged her between us up the curved tunnel.

There were other airlock covers ahead, opening and closing, keeping sealed pockets between Deepwater and deep space. We had to wait for the next one to open, fight through the blast of gas, let it close and go on to the next.

There were ten of them, opening in succession. We were tired, hardly able to keep standing, and Gret was a dead-weight between us. Her booted feet knocked over the ribbed floor. We got through two of the locks when Yoona spoke for the first time, her voice breathless as she sucked the thin air into her lungs.

'We have to follow this outflow,' she said. 'It must lead somewhere.'

It led somewhere all right.

The air smelled better now and there was more light. We tried to clean Gret's face and I felt sick when I saw where the trite-sting had gone. Yoona tore a strip off her tunic as a bandage and tied it round Gret's head. There was only a bloody patch where it crossed one eye.

We helped Gret between us for a long time. The big saucer-shaped covers opened and closed and the tunnel grew more narrow and rounded. We were slipping and sliding over the curved floor and could feel the huge engines of Deepwater pounding through the walls like a thunderous heartbeat. Once Gret began to moan sharply and we stopped until she was quiet again.

The engine-thud faded a little. Ahead was a last cover that opened and shut like biting jaws. The rounded walls of this one were set with large vents, through which the exhaust fumes streamed on their way down the tunnel. It was like being in an oven. We had to be careful because that last cover could cut us in half.

Just as we got in, the walls hummed and a blue bar of light screened over us, making the tunnel as bright as day for a moment. It was like being poked with a solid blue-white finger. Then something must have decided we were OK and not a foreign intruder to be zapped, because it switched off.

Yoona went through the cover first. Then somehow we pushed Gret through. Last, I was a bit slow and nearly got a toe snipped off.

We were in a yellow tunnel. I was getting sick of that golden colour now, but this seemed cleaner, different. There were no gases flowing and no more valves. Even the engine-beat sounded distant.

'Do you know what this is?' I whispered.

'Don't you know?'

Yoona gave me a strange look and picked up something

from the floor. It was a little red communication earring, like the one I wore.

'Reb's was missing when he came back from that last trip. I noticed it when he was prexing. I think he found his way in here.'

What did he find, I wondered? Did it blow his mind – my mind?

'Do you remember anything?'

I shook my head. No, I didn't, not even an echo.

We began going down the passage. It curved and curved and curved, twisting and looping like a giant string of mad spaghetti. Now there were tiny glints of light in the smooth, yellow walls, set like micro-crystals. First, they were scattered on their own, then in groups, circles, squares and triangles. More and more of the crystals, hundreds, then thousands and more thousands, until they were so close there was no room for patterns.

Now there was a hum of power, and flashes of different light shooting in long streams up the twisting passage, red, yellow, green, blue, purple, even mixing like electric bands of colour woven together. The passage was opening and not twisting as much.

Gret was becoming conscious again. Yoona set her down against the rounded wall very gently. She put her arms round her and spoke softly.

'Gret, we're all right. Try and relax. We'll see where this place leads. Promise, promise, we'll be back.' She kissed the top of her head. 'You saved us, thank you.'

Gret's hand met with Yoona's and they squeezed tight. But she was in too much pain and lay back, choking off another scream. North Martians hate to show any weakness. I patted her shoulder and whispered my own thanks, but she didn't move. I think she had fainted again. Yoona made her as comfortable as possible before we went on.

The passage seemed to curve endlessly up and round. The crystals were thumbnail size now, glowing and flashing in the

153

coloured light with thousands of tiny colours of their own. It was like walking underwater through a river of light.

There were fluids, too, going through thin piping in the walls. Larger pipes were overhead, some with darker fluids. Now, in the distance, we could hear a heavy pounding noise – not the Deepwater engines, but a more steady, pulse-beat noise. All the time I kept thinking I'd seen something like this before. It looked like a life-place, life-support, and I had a memory of it from somewhere on Earth. Then it came like one of those flickers of light.

'Inside a body,' I said.

'What?'

'I saw this film on telly. It was about people getting shrunk to dot-size and going into someone's body to kill a virus or something.' I looked around. 'Inside the veins, the bloodstream, was something like this.'

Yoona nodded. She understood – not about television because they didn't bother with that on Mars, but about the body. She must have been putting the same thoughts together herself.

'A life-support system,' she whispered. Gret's blood was on both our spacesuits and she tried to rub it off. 'Something being kept alive?'

Something was being kept alive. We found out what a few minutes later.

The round passage was wider, with a level floor and higher roof. Now the gleaming crystals were all over the walls in close rows. We stopped to rest and I sat down. My elbow hit the wall just on one of the crystals. There was a high, shrill screech behind me and Yoona gasped. I turned.

There before me was a horrible face floating in the air. It had a long, pointed nose and ears, sharp teeth and glinty little black eyes. It made another screechy sound and vanished.

'Audio-hologram,' said Yoona.

She reached over and pressed the crystal again. She must have pressed the next one because another face appeared, like the pointy-eared one but with a black stripe down the black fur.

I pressed one on her side. There was a faint, almost soundless, ping and a broader black and white face appeared, one that I recognised.

'That's the picture of a badger.' Yoona looked at me, puzzled. 'An Earth-animal that lived in Europe.'

We went further down the passage and pressed another crystal. This time a black and white cat miaowed at us. Then a leopard snarled. Every crystal showed a hologram when we pressed it, like a label. Zebras, antelopes and cows. The birds were the most magic because they fluttered in the air like Yoona's parrot had. All types of birds – big beaks, small beaks, all colours and shapes, a dozen at a time flapping and squawking, so real I expected them to leave something on the floor.

'It's like an index system,' said Yoona. Overhead, the fluids streamed along their pipes. 'No . . .' she was thinking now, thinking very hard. 'I've seen something like this on Mars . . . my prex memory . . . before I was sick . . .'

She shut her eyes. One by one the holograms vanished, the chattering stopped. The passage was silent except for the distant pulse-beat. Then Yoona opened her eyes and whispered two words.

'Gene bank.'

I looked at her. It made the same sense to me in the same way.

'This is a hundred times more sophisticated.' She gave a bewildered headshake. 'But it's also a hundred times better . . .'

Then I remembered something. We had fought so hard to live in the last hour that I'd forgotten. Now it flashed into my mind like a line of print on a computer screen. It was from when we were standing on the motorway silver-plate side of Deepwater, just before the spaceship shook us off. I had seen some words like graffiti, scratched into the plate by someone long dead. They may have built Deepwater in a hurry, but that unknown somebody had time for a message of hope.

'Noah had one, too.'

I whispered the words aloud. Yoona mouthed them herself in reply. Her hair was a scraggly mop round her white face.

'There's this book on Earth called the Bible—' I said.

'Yes, Robbie, we had Bibles on Mars—'

'He built an ark.'

'I know.'

Then it sank in. She leaned back sharply and somehow must have hit a crystal because a white dove fluttered overhead, cooing. Yoona looked up at it, then at me.

'Noah's ark in outer space?'

She got up and began pressing crystals, one after the other, walking down the corridor without even looking at them. More birds, then snakes hissed, turtles blinked and lizards scuttled round in a tight circle. Then a little furry thing with big ears and round eyes. Then monkeys, rows of them, all shapes and sizes. She kept pressing crystals and walking.

'Yoona!'

She stopped. A gorilla scowled grumpily at her before vanishing. The crystal rows had ended, too. Yoona looked at me and shook her head in disbelief.

'Deepwater is a gene ark.'

She was saying it to herself, not to me. And at the same time there was a flicker of something else in her face, like a question she didn't dare ask. She opened her mouth, but quickly shut it again.

'Yoona, we've got to get back to Gret.'

'Please, Robbie, just a little further.'

But there was no further. Round the next twisting corner, the gene passage ended in a rounded blank wall. There was no sign of an opening, nothing.

'That's all,' I said.

'Yes, that's all,' she said. And there was something in her voice, like a question she didn't dare ask.

'Yoona, what's the matter?'

'Nothing.' She shook her head, telling herself not to be silly. 'Let's get back to Gret. I want to get out of here.'

She walked off quickly down the corridor. I paused a moment, looking at the blank wall.

How did we get out of here?

22   *A dead crew speaks*

Gret was where we left her, the light-stream making an eddy round her huddled body. She looked up, still in pain but conscious again. She tried to get up, but Yoona put a hand on her shoulder and knelt. We told her what had happened.

'I'm surprised NUN didn't try and get you,' she whispered.

Yoona shook her head. 'I don't think even NUN can get in here,' she said.

Then she took the red earring communicator from her pocket and held it out.

'Reb did.' She looked at me. 'And not through the exhaust tunnel either.'

I shook my head. I had no memory and after my last prex, that little Reb-echo seemed to have gone. But it didn't seem to matter now, because we'd been crawling all through Deepwater and knew more about it – about the people who built it, how they thought and planned.

'The gene bank was sealed,' said Yoona softly. 'But the people who built it . . . would need a way in themselves . . . for an emergency.'

'A way that nothing else could use,' said Gret, a hand over her eye.

'The light,' I said. That bar of blue-white light that probed us in the last tunnel section. 'It didn't hurt us because we were human—'

'But anything else would get sizzled – yes!' Yoona grinned with excitement. 'Come on.'

Gret could move now. The trap clicked shut behind us and

the blue-white light hissed over again. It held us a moment the way you hold a butterfly, with the strength to crush us. And above, in the shadowed curve of the tunnel ceiling was another of those metal airlock traps. It opened at a touch and through it, the rungs of a steel ladder led up into the shadows above.

I went up first while Yoona helped Gret up and followed. Gret made a little gasp in biting off the pain, but she went up the ladder by herself. One of those automatic lights came on as we reached the top.

We must have been right at the top of Deepwater as on the backbone of a whale. A long, narrow walkway stretched ahead as far as we could see, ending in shadows. And the light showed us something else, a message scrawled in bold letters on the dust of the wall: REB. DEEPWATER.

He had come this way and had found the gene bank. But the shock must have been too much and somehow triggered a prex cycle he never escaped.

I shivered. I was here on Deepwater because of that and I felt really close to my other self then. He was a real explorer, afraid of nothing. No wonder Yoona valued him so much and no wonder I blinked back tears.

'Come on, Robbie,' she said. There were tears in her voice.

We began walking along the passage. It must have been the final section built, and scribbled graffiti scratched in the metal walls wrote the last chapter in the puzzle of Deepwater.

'MY FAMILY GROUP ALL GONE – CELA WROTE THIS.' Then, further on, 'MEMORY OF ULAN, DEAD SPIKE-VIRUS.' And in a larger, childish hand, 'NO MORE MISTAKES – BETTER NEXT TIME, PLEASE.'

I remembered those people in the streaming rain, how they just collapsed as the virus took them. They all kept working until the last, even the children. On the floor was a little rag-doll. It crumbled to dust when Yoona touched it.

The automatic lights were going on in sections, showing the way ahead and closing in shadows behind. We must have been walking for an hour and Gret was swaying on her feet.

We stopped again, and as we did another section of lights went on. Ahead was a closed metal door.

'Let's go on,' whispered Gret.

Exhausted though she was, she took the first step forward. North Martians were tough, very tough. The door had an ordinary handle and swung open with a loud squeal that made us all jump. I went inside and Yoona followed with Gret.

We were inside another control room and from the curve of the ceiling, it must have been above ours. There was no observation window and only four of the black metal chairs. The walls and top were made of that silver-glass plate. It was see-through from this side and the light turned the deep black of outer space into dark blue.

'I've never seen this on those lay-out grids,' said Gret.

Neither had I. But COL hadn't shown us the gene bank on its grid-patterns either. Yoona was leading Gret over to one of the chairs – then she stopped.

Each chair had a crumpled silver-grey track suit on it, adult size. They were not standing like those space suits in the other ship. These looked as though they had been laid down . . . like someone sitting. Then we knew what we were looking at.

All that was left of the first Deepwater crew.

They had been here so many thousand years that even their bones had become dust inside the imperishable material of their track suits. One suit had a glove missing – we had found its pair on the main deck. Their names were stencilled above the pockets like ours. 'KANER' and 'ERL' were the two nearest. On the far side, the other two names made me catch my breath. 'BARLA' and 'TEM'.

Yoona's parents. She went over and stood looking at them. In Barla's limp glove was a small journal disc. Yoona took it very gently from the empty fingers and pressed the milled edge. Barla's voice filled the silent, dark room. It was deep and good-sounding, and gasped a little as though she was very tired.

'Yoona, our daughter. The virus came with us on the ship. Death is near. One day you will hear this, you will know who

161

you are and what your mission is from NUN. Our love to you and the others. All are special. Good fortune on the other side. No more mistakes.' The voice gasped a little and repeated the last three words with a faint, desperate stress. 'No more mistakes. Live as one. Goodbye my darling.'

Yoona didn't cry or anything like that. She slipped the disc in her pocket and, leaning over, touched each black-lettered name. Her lips trembled, but she looked proud.

It was so plain now what had happened. Tem, Barla and the other two, Kaner and Erl, had guided Deepwater on the first stage of its journey out of Earth's solar system. Then they had programmed COL for the island galaxies, probably checked the gene bank one more time and set NUN with our genes. And when they had done all this, they came back up here to this little upper cabin and waited to die.

'We always thought NUN and COL ran Deepwater.' Yoona's voice was low. 'But we were always meant to be the real crew.'

NUN's task was to clone and educate the next crew of Deepwater from gene cells, producing perfect identical copies of the real kids whose bodies they had been taken from. But NUN was a thinking machine and maybe more than that. Maybe thoughts bring their own emotions. NUN wouldn't tell us everything and even though an automatic programming released us at the right age, NUN wanted us back – just like those parents who can never let their kids leave home.

And Barla's message. What had she meant by the 'other side' and 'no more mistakes'? We should have known, but we didn't because the bio-computer that gave us life tried to play God.

Another door led to narrow, metal stairs, going down and set with landings. A space-helmet lay on one, covered with dust. At the bottom was another airlock hatch and the same solid bar of blue-white light hummed over us. The hatch was part of the ceiling-light housing in the first airlock chamber – that was why we'd never noticed it. Neat. If the light didn't zap an intruder, it could be blown out of the airlock. The people who planned Deepwater really had thought of everything.

Except perhaps of NUN spending the next hundred thousand years thinking about itself and getting more and more possessive.

We dropped into the airlock chamber. Gret was nearly fainting again and we were almost as bad. Too much had happened and the last part, that silent, dusty cabin, was even worse than going up the airlock tunnel. No wonder Reb had prexed. But we were back, knowing a lot more about Deepwater and ourselves – even Bren would be pleased. Yoona punched the airlock button and the door slid open.

It seemed like most of our troubles were over.

Lis was still below deck and Zak was sitting on the stairs. They gave us a look of horror and Zak yelled through the open hatch. Bren came running down as we laid Gret on the bed. We didn't hear him shout to COL or anything. And he always looked so full of himself, but now he was pale, washed out. It wasn't just the sight of Gret. Something else had happened. He watched silently while Yoona gave Gret a pain-killer.

'Bren, status report.' She was commander again.

He was still looking at Gret and didn't seem to hear her. Then he shook his head wearily as though nothing mattered.

'Nobody has control of Deepwater,' he said.

Yoona headed for the stairs, fast. I forgot how tired I was and followed.

Everything was quiet on the main deck and the space outside was total black. No colour, no meteors, not even stars now. Just complete blackness. And there was something strange about the way Deepwater wasn't moving.

Yoona put her hand on the console and shouted for COL. Nothing. The console didn't glow red. She tried again.

'COL!'

There was no answer. COL was gone. We'd lived with that voice for so long, we just took it for granted. Bren was coming up the stairs and Yoona gave him a furious look.

'You must have blown the circuits!'

'No! COL wouldn't even let us turn Deepwater round. It blocked all our commands and then shut down.'

'Shut down?'

'Yes. COL announced it – shutting down. And did.'

I was looking out of the main observation port. In the very far distance there was a set of faint long lines in space, like crack marks on the black bowl.

'When did you see those?' I asked.

Bren was pale and very quiet. 'About the same time COL shut down. None of our screening makes any sense of it.'

I picked up on Deepwater's 'motion' again. There was a strange movement as though the spaceship was moving very gently. Once, on a camping trip, I'd chucked a twig into the river. It had floated for a time and the current had slowly drawn it out into midstream. And that was how Deepwater was moving now, as though something powerful was beginning to pull it gently.

Lis and Zak came up. Gret was asleep. Yoona told them what had happened and she kept nothing back – how to open the NUN door, the gene bank, that other cabin. And she played Barla's journal disc.

'So we can get back to NUN now,' Zak said.

Zak's voice was harsh and tense. Bren and Lis had listened in silence but he'd fidgeted, standing on one leg, then the other, looking restless. I think he'd stopped listening to everything after the NUN door, even Barla's voice. We looked at him.

'Don't you see? COL stopped because NUN told him to. All we have to do is ask NUN, ask him like we used to.'

'Zak, NUN's solid-holograms can't help us get Deepwater started. We have to figure out what that thing is.'

That 'thing' was a little closer. The crack marks seemed to stretch for ever in either direction and looked real and solid, not like something floating. And Deepwater was moving now, very slowly but already seeming to pick up speed.

'I think we're caught in some kind of forcefield,' whispered Yoona.

'NUN will help us,' came Zak's voice from behind.

'Zak,' I said. 'We've been there. NUN is just—'

Zak had gone downstairs and returned with a laser rifle. He was pointing it at us.

'I'm going to ask NUN. If anyone tries to stop me, I'll use this.'

He spun round and ran down the stairs. We followed. Below deck, Zak was already at the NUN door. His hand flickered over the controls and the door began to swing open. On the bed, Gret stirred restlessly.

'Zak, no!' shouted Lis.

He was already running through the door. Bren grabbed a laser rifle and Yoona pulled it out of his hands.

'We can't start shooting each other!' She looked round, thinking. 'Bren, stay on deck, please.'

He nodded. Yoona grabbed my arm and we ran through the door, Lis behind us. Already a long way ahead of us down the passage ran Zak, in a crazy, long-legged way. He turned and swung the rifle, screaming at us.

'Back!'

Maybe the rifle went off by accident, because the laser bolt hit the ceiling. Red-hot metal splattered round us and we ducked. Zak was already at the other door. It opened and the golden light seemed to clutch round his body with thick, greedy arms. It seemed like he was pulled in. Yoona stopped and turned to Lis.

'Understand, Lis, I don't think you should go in there.'

'Yoona, Zak is my friend, he needs help—'

'Please, Lis. I do know what I'm talking about.'

Lis nodded. Yoona and I pushed open the door and plunged back into that golden haze. All the same fantastic clutter of beautiful and incredible stuff was there, but this time we could kick it aside. It was solid but not real. At first we couldn't see Zak, but then we heard his voice. He was begging and crying, happy and sobbing like he'd really cracked up. And through his voice ran the soothing, syrupy, yellow tones of NUN.

'NUN!' Yoona stopped and shouted. 'Let him go! You have to let us all go!'

'You must all come back to me, Yoona.' The yellow voice just flowed on as though she hadn't spoken.

'We will, NUN,' cried Zak. 'Deepwater has stopped, not moving.'

'Deepwater?' said NUN and stopped, as though realising the mistake.

'Yes, Deepwater!' shouted Yoona. 'Mastermind, you don't even know the name of our spaceship!'

NUN's globe seemed to flush a deeper yellow.

'So tell us what amebs are, NUN!' Yoona was shouting – I'd never seen her so bitter and angry. 'Tell us about trites, about the people who built this spaceship – tell us who we *are*!'

Nothing came from the NUN ball. It still had deep yellow flushes as if it were angry – or confused.

'NUN can if it wants to,' said Zak, but he looked up uncertainly.

'Then why doesn't it answer?' I shouted.

'Because NUN has nothing to say. Nothing to offer but toys!'

'No, Yoona!' Zak was desperate. 'NUN can do anything!'

'Listen to it, Zak.' Yoona was inching closer. 'Can you hear anything? NUN is a bio-computer that got its programming wrong.'

'No, Yoona!' The golden voice was strong – but upset, I could sense that. 'Not wrong to be lonely.' It seemed to echo a note of sadness.

'Wrong to hold us here,' said Yoona. Her anger was gone. 'You can't help us now. Gret has lost her eye because of a trite. You could make a solid-hologram of that trite, so real it would drill the other one out. But you couldn't make her a new eye. That's no use to us.'

The NUN ball was flushing deep yellow to orange now, like someone's face turning red with anger.

'NUN can save us,' said Zak. The laser rifle was hanging limp in his hands.

'No!' Yoona and I were closer. She looked up again. 'NUN can't even save itself.'

She looked up and her voice was full of strength and scorn.

'NUN, you don't need us. If you haven't got enough toys to play with, make some more.'

NUN had flushed to deep orange and was silent. But the waves of colour beat on us like hot emotion. Then, behind Zak, the Roman statue seemed to shift and look at him. One of the throne chairs moved as though somebody invisible had sat on it. Some moonstones rolled over the floor as though kicked and behind Zak I saw something that made my blood run cold.

The crystal door was open and a thick tongue of jel had slid quietly into the NUN-room, pushing everything aside, building up the rugs before it like a multicoloured wave. It was headed straight for us. Yoona saw it at the same time.

'Zak! Behind you!'

The laser rifle jerked up in his hands as he looked round. Then he giggled and looked up at the orange-flushing NUN ball overhead.

'No, that will not hurt us, that is part of NUN. We will all be part of NUN.'

Behind him, the jel grew into a slobbery red mass, panting and snuffling towards us.

23 The other side

'Zak!' I yelled and took another step towards him.

'Stay where you are! Don't move!' He giggled again. 'Soon we will all be with NUN.'

The golden light reflected off his eyes and streamed down his body like he was a puppet pulled by yellow strings.

Something moved at my side and I turned. Lis had come in. She was overwhelmed by the golden light but still moving, hands out like she was sleepwalking – sleepwalking with her eyes full of life.

The slobbery red jel-mass was closer. Zak stood there, the laser on us, letting the stuff creep up. Overhead the NUN ball was flushing back from orange to yellow.

'Soon,' said Zak. 'We will all be in the body of NUN.'

'Zak, that stuff will eat you!'

Lis's voice was desperate. Zak looked at her, his eyes wild.

'Get back, Lis,' Yoona said.

Lis had already moved past us. Her chubby blue face was set in scared but resolute lines as she got behind Zak, still moving as though underwater. The yellow-orange light poured a solid river down on her and behind, the jel swelled and swelled. Zak seemed to register for the first time.

'Lis, get away.'

Lis stood there. She pressed her lips in a tight line.

'The jel will have to get me first.'

She was so scared her teeth chattered but she stood there as the jel-wave built higher than her, faster and faster. She shot a look behind and gave a small cry of panic but stood there, trembling, eyes shut, waiting.

Zak was watching, glaring. Then suddenly the yellow light wasn't reflecting in his eyes and he swung the laser rifle up fast and fired directly into the globe. There was a huge golden explosion and a circle of light blasted down like a yellow sledge-hammer. Zak was smashed to the floor. Round us came a loud whistling, screaming noise like energy released or something in pain. The exploded bits of the NUN ball floated in the golden air and began falling. The jel-wave swelled and rippled.

'Lis, run!' I yelled.

She did, but the jel was already over her and toppling. Then the yellow light seemed to fade and the jel quivered and stopped. Lis ran clear, then stopped and looked round.

So did Yoona and I. The NUN chamber, the treasure-room of Deepwater, was changing. Everything was flickering and dotting, speckled with light. Lis took a header over one of the throne chairs, but a moment later it fell on her, through her and disappeared. Everything was transparent, fading.

Lis's little sand-diver hopped up, puzzled. It blinked big eyes at her and vanished. The tumbled wave-pattern of rugs was also disappearing. In the centre the white statue was last, body glimmering in the air.

The yellow in the air faded as the forcefield went. The air cleared and the eight rain-crystal caskets were left on their own.

'Zak – Zak!'

Yoona and I knelt, but Lis pushed us back. She put her arms round Zak and hugged him tight like her own body would bring him back to life. Yoona put a gentle hand on Zak's wrist, feeling for a pulse. Nothing. But Lis held and held, the tears streaming down her cheeks.

Zak lay still, his eyes shut. He looked peaceful, almost sleeping. At the very last, the artificial love of NUN could not take over from the real thing he felt for his crewmates, especially for Lis.

Everything was cold in the NUN chamber now and the

yellow walls had faded to their natural metal grey. Lis hugged Zak even tighter and still cried. Yoona and I put our arms round her and let the four of us lock together. I don't know how much time passed before we picked up Zak and carried him over to the caskets. We opened his and put him inside. Lis crossed his arms and gave him a last kiss, whispering something in his ear.

Yoona looked up. 'COL,' she said, 'I don't know if you can still hear us or if you have the power to do this. But please try and do something for Zak. Whatever you can.' There was no sound from overhead, no answer. Lis lowered the casket lid and Yoona set the controls in the base to seal it. We could still see Zak's face through the thick rain-crystal and he looked peaceful. He had woken up in that casket not even a year ago and now he was back inside – sleeping again, we hoped.

The only other thing in the NUN chamber was the wave-thing of jel. It had gone a browny-black and large cracks were showing as though it was becoming dry and crumbling. It must have been part of NUN. Maybe a bio-computer has its own generating mass or something, I thought. NUN must have used its mass to try and get us back, make us part of it. I think it was as simple as that and as sad, because even a thinking computer had nothing to give us but make-believe.

Bren had come in. He walked over, looking at the crumbling mass of jel and at NUN's closed casket. He didn't look tough now, just awkward and sad.

'I'm sorry, Lis. It was my fault.' At least he admitted that. She just nodded.

'Not all your fault, Bren,' said Yoona, 'and I told you to stay on deck.'

'You'd better come and look.'

We did. Yoona slammed the NUN door behind her and we returned to the upper deck.

The broken-bowl cracks were much closer and wider. They seemed to spread round on both sides and the centre looked as through something had blasted through the blackness, like a

171

stone through a window. 'Black holes' and 'wormholes' Denie had talked about; a time-speeding metro system of the universe. Was this a pocket of space like that? Whatever it was, Deepwater was moving more quickly, like a twig hitting the current. And we were ants on the back of the twig.

COL was silent and the console cold. There seemed to be flashing streaks in the cracks, like strobe lighting. The jagged hole in the centre became bigger and bigger. Deepwater was caught in a force, pulling it faster and faster.

We were all quiet. There was nothing we could do. We slept in our chairs, on and off. Gret was on deck in hers, and Lis knelt between Yoona and me. She hadn't spoken since we put Zak in the casket. There was nothing else round us, not even a stray meteorite or distant star; even Colour-space was far behind. We were alone and flooded in darkness. Deepwater, the huge spaceship, was a floating matchstick in this black ocean.

'So what'll happen when we get to that hole?' said Lis. She sounded like she didn't care.

'We'll get pulled in,' I said. And it didn't take any brains to know that. Deepwater was moving faster and faster and we could hear a faint roaring sound vibrating through the spaceship.

'Pulled in to where?' said Bren.

'Wherever it is, it was meant to happen.' Yoona had her mother's journal disc on a cord round her neck. On both sides was that circle-diagram with the V-notch at the top. She was looking at it like a memory was sparking. 'Deepwater has been on a set course and this is where it was heading.'

'Into nothing?' said Gret.

'Into something,' said Yoona. Her eyes opened wide and she knew, that was when she *knew*.

She made to speak again, but Deepwater shuddered and began moving faster. Even space itself seemed to be rushing past like a black windstorm. The vibrating roar was louder and Yoona raised her voice.

'The other side.'

'The universe goes in a circle,' I said. Denie's words, not mine, but they flashed up automatically.

Yoona looked at me and nodded. The black current-roaring was even faster and Yoona ordered us to strap into our seats. Lis clung to the back of hers. The jagged splinter-hole was much closer now, bigger than our spaceship, and about to swallow us like a monster mouth. I could only just hear Yoona speak.

'I know where we're going.'

The roaring suddenly deafened us. Deepwater lurched again, like going down a plug-hole. We clung to the seats and each other as the spaceship stood on its head and dived into the swirling darkness. It was like being flung into the middle of a black, storming whirlpool, down and down, faster and faster, into a black, bottomless nothing.

Then the blackness crunched into us like a solid concrete wall. Deepwater crashed so hard it nearly came apart. Huge black ocean waves were smashing against our sides like battering-rams, we were caught and spinning like a plastic toy in the bath. Then the waves froze over solid, holding us in a cold, black nothing. Not the emptiness of outer space, but the nothing of nothing.

The lights on Deepwater dimmed, and a freezing cold went through the ship like an icy hand clutching tight. Beside me, Yoona made herself relax in her seat. Her voice echoed in the darkness.

'We'll come out of this. I think we know all the secrets of Deepwater.'

'Then where are we going?' gasped Lis. She was clinging to the back of Yoona's chair, her teeth chattering.

'Around the circle of the universe. And time-blinking thousands of years forwards.' Her finger traced the V in the circle-design. 'That V-shape is here, the break in the circle like a black hole. We go through and end our journey.'

Nobody spoke. We were freezing with the cold and the

173

dimming yellow lights of Deepwater made the outside even blacker.

'Planet Earth was dying of pollution. But there must have been gene banks of Earth-life on the Martian colonies for the terraforming, to make the new world. But it was too late for the colonies, too. So they built two Deepwater spaceships and put gene banks on them.'

'Taking them where?' asked Gret.

Yoona smiled in the dimming light. 'Where else do you take the gene bank of Planet Earth – but home?'

A loud cracking noise suddenly terrified us; it sounded like the iron-glass splintering. But it was the frozen blackness itself, splitting into a spider's web outside. Then all round, everything shattered into thousands of pieces. For another long minute nothing happened, then Deepwater jerked sideways and broke clear, like an iceberg splashing back into the black water of outer space.

At the same time there was a slight ringing sound in the air and Yoona shouted, 'COL?'

The console glowed red. 'Awaiting instructions.'

'COL, why did you shut down?' Yoona couldn't help smiling with relief.

'Pre-flight programming order.' And that was all COL said. Maybe that plunge into nothing had to be natural, none of us allowed to interfere.

'Yoona . . .' Lis had already forgotten about COL. 'Planet Earth is dead, there's nothing to go home to.'

'No. I think all these thousands of years, Earth will have been cleaning itself. The way a planet can if it's left alone. I think it's ready for life again.'

Yoona unstrapped herself from her chair. What she said was so simple and obvious that we had to believe. We had gone round the universe to bring life back to our solar system.

'Look,' said Bren. 'Is that Earth?'

Ahead, suspended in the far distant blackness, was a planet with a single moon.

174

Yoona took a deep breath. 'Gret, scan for life readings.'

Gret winced a little as she leaned forwards. Her quick fingers raced over the keyboard and the hologram readouts flickered up. Gret looked at them with disbelief and began to input again.

'Gret, what is it?' Lis was yelling with panic. Nothing could go wrong now!

Gret was looking at her readouts, then at the planet, and she groaned. Not from pain, but despair.

'None—' she choked, and went on, 'none of the readouts show any signs of life-support, air, earth, water . . . anything.'

'Do them again,' said Yoona.

Gret already was. Her bandage slipped and she pushed it back up again. There was silence on the deck, but we all knew the truth before she spoke. It was in the long, hopeless sigh she gave.

'That planet is dead. Dead.'

24   Decision into darkness

Gret did the readings a third time. They came up exactly the same. There was nothing to indicate life on that planet-sized lump of dead rock. It looked grey and beaten.

'The end . . .' said Lis.

I felt more to blame than the others. My generation could have stopped all this. Then I looked again and thought of something so obvious that I felt really stupid.

'Hey, where's the sun?'

Gret inputted again and gave a cry of astonishment. 'I don't get this. The sun is about six billion kilometres away. Earth is much closer.' She flashed up a star chart. 'It should be only about a hundred and fifty million kilometres—'

She had been putting a navigational fix into her console. She had forgotten her pain. The readout flickered and she leaned back. I have seen Gret look arrogant, rude and even hurt. But I had never seen her look silly. Until now.

'That's Pluto,' she said.

'That's the wrong planet, Gret,' said Lis. 'No wonder we can't see the sun.'

Gret just sat there. It was strange watching a green-faced girl go red with embarrassment and I felt sorry for her.

'Don't worry, Gret, the time-warp or whatever it was would have been for our solar system, not Earth itself—' That was as far as I got.

'All right, all right,' she flashed, as sharp as ever. 'I suppose Earthkids never made mistakes, did they, Robbie?'

I was too relieved to bite back. And anyway, it was the

first time she'd called me Robbie.

'COL, course for Planet Earth please,' said Yoona, a hand over her mouth. 'Maximum speed.'

COL's fastest speed for Deepwater was time-blinking and the spaceship shuddered. A black fast-forward of space whizzed past. Uranus, Neptune, Saturn, Jupiter ... after crossing the billion billion kilometres of the universe, Deepwater moved through this backyard like a jet-propelled shark. Yoona slowed Deepwater at Ceres and again at Mars, but it was no use. The same readouts came as Pluto flickered up. South and North Martian kids stood together as their planet glided past.

Another shudder and time-blink of super-speed. Earth was the next planet. Yoona slowed Deepwater again and Gret put her hands on the console. She paused, like an executioner holding the axe, then flicked the readouts into operation.

It was too soon. We were too far away. We had to wait and wait as the planet grew, blocked by its moon. We all stood together and Yoona slipped her hand into mine. All of us shared the last long, long minute as the Moon slipped away and Earth filled our screen and windows.

And we knew straight away, at the first glance, because Earth was a huge round globe, splashed with green, white and blue, glowing like a healthy, happy face at us. And the readouts chattered like all the birds sleeping in our gene banks.

'Water density ... air density ... land mass ... life sustaining ...'

Gret stopped speaking and the tears came from her single good eye. Bren knelt beside her and pulled one of his dreadlocks hard. And Lis, happy tears this time, blue on her blue cheeks. Tears down my cheeks, too, and only Yoona was dry-eyed. But it was the proudest moment of her life.

'No more mistakes,' she breathed.

She wasn't talking to us, but repeating Barla's words on the journal disc round her neck. I was angry about my tears, then I thought to hell with it, I should be crying because what we had done was so incredible. Below were the blue oceans with a white scribble of clouds over them. Then the darker colours of land-mass and everything looked beautiful, bright and new.

This time we had to make it work.

Then Yoona rubbed her hand down her face and some of that doubt, that question-mark, came back into her eyes. She paused another long minute before speaking.

'COL, do you have a set program for release of the gene bank?'

'Yes.'

'COL. Commence program.' Then she stiffened in her seat and spoke again, sharply. 'COL, can we monitor?'

'Yes.'

Our giant, curved vision screen flickered on. Deepwater was speeding up and going into a closer circle round the green, white and blue planet below. I couldn't recognise anything. In a million years, continents and countries had changed. There was just one land-mass at the bottom of the southern ocean.

Now Deepwater was closer and speeding very quickly. A heavy, vibrating thud ran through the spaceship as machinery, a long time not used, came to life. Yoona sat there, stiff and tense, looking at the vision screen.

I don't know how COL had been programmed to do it or even how the genes would activate into life. I suppose twenty-first century hi-tech had thought of all that – what was released first, what got down to the surface first. As we orbited, we could look back and see a wake of tiny, gleaming capsules being shed behind us like rainbow circles, then began to drift down like leaves.

As they did, the vision screen flashed. It seemed to start with tiny marine life, then bigger, then fish, seaweed, shells, thousands of images going past in micro-seconds, then trees and plants, insects, the sudden flutter of a million butterfly wings, the snakes, reptiles, the small mammals. They were images from COL's memory-banks, matching each set of genes leaving the spaceship.

As Deepwater turned, we could see larger versions of those

179

round capsules appearing as the bigger life-forms went down. Lions, tigers, a whole mixture of animal faces so quick we could scarcely pick out the main ones: elephant, giraffe, zebra, birds, monkeys, ending with that gorilla face I'd seen as a hologram in the gene bank – the one that made me think of Meatgrinder, a million years away on the other side of time. The vision screen went blank and COL spoke.

'Gene stock ejection ended.'

We all sat in silence. It was like watching the best movie in the world and not wanting it to end. The last outer rings of the glittering circles were sinking down into the atmosphere like rainbow seeds. How life would start, and how they worked, we could not even begin to guess. Beside me, though, Yoona was sitting rigid. She didn't look happy, more like a horrible nightmare was happening.

'COL, is that all?'

'Program completed.'

Now everyone was looking at her, picking up on that desperate sound in her voice.

'COL, are the gene banks empty?'

'Empty.'

'No!' She stood up and for the first time she shouted at COL like a mother screaming at her kid. 'COL, we have a gene bank of Planet Earth, that can't be all.'

'My gene bank stops at the lower primates.'

Yoona was going very pale. But I think this was something she had known and just never dared tell herself. Now we were all realising it, and why she was so – so terrified.

The lower primates. The monkeys and apes, ending with the gorillas. It was so horrible and simple that none of us had even thought about it, except Yoona. Maybe humans are like that, always taking themselves for granted. But the gene banks were empty and the truth was staring at us from that blank vision screen.

'The other Deepwater.' Gret was the first to put it into whispered words.

The other Deepwater. Two spaceships and two clone crews. Back-up for each other, we had thought, in case one didn't make it. But that wasn't the reason. One held a careful cross-section of genes for the animal kingdom. The other held another cross-section of genes just as carefully selected – for the human race.

That Deepwater we had left broken and drifting in space was the human gene ark, now lost forever at the other end of the universe.

'That was what the other NUN was trying to tell me,' said Yoona. 'I had a feeling . . .'

She had her eyes tight shut as she remembered. I recalled how she'd run through our gene bank, stabbing at those crystals. She'd been looking for a single human face.

'We . . . we were in the forcefield of the time-warp . . . by the time I knew.'

Deepwater went into a holding pattern. We were safe back in our galaxy, far away from the alien monsters of the outer colour-jungle. So we got up. Gret, Bren and Lis went below to rest. I wandered round the deck. Yoona sat in the control chair, elbows on knees, hands over her face and blonde hair tangled in her fingers. She didn't move for an hour and I knew she was blaming herself. And all that time we went round and round Planet Earth below, the planet that was now beginning the miracle of life. And we could never land.

Even I knew it was impossible. We six kids in a strange new world couldn't start the human race again by ourselves. Denie had told me about inbreeding when she told me about genes. It was all so stupid and horrible. It was like we'd won a really important match, then been told we didn't even know what the game was about. That human gene ark must have been a cross-section of everything that was best. We felt the loss of all those people. That rainbow arch above the broken ship . . . the tombstone of the human race in outer space.

Yoona moved in her chair and spoke into the intercom.

'Everybody on deck please.' She looked at me, her face expressionless and calm. She'd come to a decision.

They came up and Yoona turned to the console. 'COL, are the gene bank capsules on the other Deepwater the same as ours?'

'Yes.'

'How long can they survive in outer space?'

'Indefinitely.'

She looked at us and we all knew what she was thinking. It was so incredible, we forget everything else.

'COL, can you put us into a suspended animation in our caskets?'

'Yes.'

She looked at us defiantly, but her voice shook. 'COL, can you take Deepwater on the same route again?' Her voice shook again. 'Across the universe?'

'Yes.'

Yoona stood up and faced us. Behind her, through the eye-windows, was the big patchwork globe of Planet Earth. There were faint rainbow lines still round it. She began speaking, but stopped as her voice broke. She took a deep breath.

'I don't like asking you this. I don't want to spend the rest of my life on this spaceship. I'd rather be down there with the new life. But if there's one chance of saving the gene bank . . . we have to try.'

Gret, Bren and Lis looked at each other. Then Gret spoke in her abrupt, sour-apples way. 'And if we don't, I suppose our brave South Martian commander will fly across the universe alone.'

'Not alone,' I said. I stood beside Yoona.

Bren curled his lip. 'She's got her Earthkid. So she won't need a rockhead Jupie then.'

'Or a sandbrain,' said Lis. There was a strange look on her face, like she was angry and laughing at the same time.

Yoona couldn't believe it. 'None of you!'

'What do you think we were talking about below?' said Gret.

'We've already decided to come' – her voice broke a moment – 'you silly, stupid Py-poppie.'

'Try and stop us,' growled Bren.

Yoona just put out her hands. We all joined each other in a circle with no break in it. We were truly united and it was the best, most wonderful feeling ever. Even Gret laughed and kissed Yoona – yes, Gret, I wished I had a camera. We hugged each other and went on hugging. Even Bren was grinning like a kid.

'COL.' Yoona's voice burst with pride. 'We are going back across the universe.'

'Yes, Yoona.'

It was the first time COL had ever spoken a name. So even COL approved and it was only a computer. Or maybe not because before we'd been wrong about a lot of things. But now we knew we had made the right decision. We were the crew of Deepwater and it was our job to go.

That was two Earth-days ago. There were a lot of preparations for the journey, although at least COL knows the way. I am finishing this journal-log because soon it will be my turn to go into that empty NUN chamber to lie down in the casket with the crystal cover.

Gret and Bren went a little time ago. They didn't say goodbye, because none of us is saying goodbye. Lis managed a quick handwave before she marched bravely down the passage. She wants the casket beside Zak. Maybe one day he would wake up again or we would all go on sleeping together.

We are back over Mars. We have done one low orbit under the cloud cover, but there is no sign of life. The pyramid-sets in the Hellas basin are stripped down to nothing. There were hundreds of those scaly humanoid things I'd seen in the prex on them, and the spike-flowers were already growing over. There is no human life anywhere in the solar system except us.

Now Deepwater is back in the same starting position of so long ago. Billions of kilometres ahead are the dangers of Colour-space, and there may be no life on that spaceship anyway. We can feel our Deepwater stretching itself like a marathon runner with a long race ahead. Yoona gave COL final instructions before we went up into the bubble-room for a last look at the star that was Planet Earth.

'Yoona, what do you think happened on that other Deepwater?'

'I don't know. Our crew nearly turned on us, and maybe the same thing happened there. Maybe their NUN made the same mistakes. Maybe they just wanted to get out of it.'

So did they put their leaders back in the caskets and try to leave? Were those empty space suits all the trites had left? Perhaps the answers were waiting for us in the wreckage. So long as some of their gene cargo was.

I thought about myself and the other Robbie. 'Other Robbie', that was how I was thinking about him now. An Earthkid gene that they had somehow programmed with the memory and appearance of a South Martian boy. But the Earth-gene memory was stronger and had broken through. And because he was a good kid with a good friend, Denie Miles, there was life back on Earth. And even the human race had a chance.

Earth was just another star in the blackness. We went below to the main deck. 'I'll go now,' I said, trying to be as casual as I could.

'OK, Robbie.' Yoona was trying to be casual too. I gave her the same brave smile Lis gave us and headed for the hatch, but turned again as she called after me.

'Robbie?' She was over by the control chair, the blackness of deep space through the eye-windows behind her. 'They knew what they were doing, putting an Earthkid's gene on board, didn't they?'

Her words tuned exactly with my thoughts. I shook my head. 'I don't know why.'

'I think it was to kick ass. You came along at just the right time.'

I wanted to go over and hug her tight. She wanted to hug me, too, but that was wrong, too much like saying goodbye.

And we weren't saying goodbye, just goodnight.

She paused, looking out the window into black space. 'Do you mind if I call you Reb?'

'No, I'd like that.' In fact I felt a bit proud.

'Thanks. For everything.'

'See you in the morning, Yoona.'

'In the morning, Reb.'

She smiled and sat down. The console glowed red under her hand. I turned and went down the stairs. It was a long lonely walk to the NUN chamber, but I had a good picture in my mind to keep me going – Yoona sitting at the controls of her spaceship, turning Deepwater outward on its second journey to the stars.